Sunset Mantle

SUNSET MANTLE

Alter S. Reiss

A TOM DOHERTY ASSOCIATES BOOK

NEW YORK

SUNSET MANTLE

Copyright © 2015 by Alter S. Reiss

Cover art copyright © 2015 by Richard Anderson

Edited by Carl Engle-Laird

A Tor.com Book

Published by Tom Doherty Associates, LLC

175 Fifth Avenue

New York, NY 10010

www.tor.com

Tor* is a registered trademark of Tom Doherty Associates, LLC.

ISBN 978-1-4668-9188-3 (e-book)

ISBN 978-0-7653-8521-5 (trade paperback)

First Edition: September 2015

For Israel and Myriam Reiss, for Uriel, and for Naomi

Sunset Mantle

Chapter 1

It was a heavy wool mantle dyed black and lined with rabbit fur, the sort of cloak that might be worn by a captain at arms, or a prosperous merchant. The embroidery followed all around the edge of the cloak, all the reds and oranges and yellows of a sunset close threaded, twisting up until here and there the dark shape of a swallow could be seen. Farther up the mantle, there were more birds, and more, until the embroidered birds could not be distinguished from the black of dyed wool. It was the finest thing Cete had ever seen.

He stood there, in the street leading out of Reach Antach, looking at the mantle hanging beside the door of the seamstress's shop, reaching out to touch it, and then pulling back, his fingers clumsy and blunt beside the glory of that cloak.

"Is there some help I can give you?" asked a woman coming out from the inside of the shop.

Cete turned like a startled cat. It had been time out of memory since someone had come upon him unawares. He had been so lost in the embroidery that he had neglected even the most basic caution.

The woman did not start back at his turn, just waited, with the same questioning look on her face.

"It is remarkable work," said Cete, finding his voice.

"The mantle, you mean?" she replied. "Thank you. It is three years of stitching. A commission; bought, but not paid for."

Cete looked again at the mantle, at the sunset, at the cloud of swallows rising up into the sunset. Even if he could afford it, it was not for him. It was beautiful, and it had looked like he could have it, but it was already gone. Much like the Reach Antach. It seemed a fine place, but Cete was sure it had already been given over to slaughter.

"I would give a great deal to own something so fine," he said.

"Mm?" asked the woman.

Without thinking, without looking away from the mantle, Cete unhitched his belt. "Would this be sufficient?" he said, passing it over. "I cannot ask for a thing that has been sold, but . . . perhaps this could . . ."

"No," she said. "No; this is of no use to me, and of great value to you. I cannot take it."

Cete looked away from the mantle to see the woman. She was holding the belt, running her hands over the links. "The workmanship is no better than serviceable," he said, "but it is not flawed. And there is the value of the silver, and the clasp and the boss are stamped; surely—"

"It is a merit chain from the prince of the Hainst clan," she said. "Since I did not earn it, I could take no pride in what it is. The silver value is too much less than the chain's true worth. This is of no use to me."

As she talked, she held the belt out, but did not look at it. She didn't look directly at Cete, either. Her clouded eyes rested a bit to the left of where she should be looking. Blind. Blind, but she could make a thing like that cloak. Blind, but she wore her hair in the braids of an unmarried woman, not loose like an outcast, and her shop was near the center of the Reach, not beyond the walls.

During the afternoon services, Cete had seen the Antach of the Antach speaking to a tribal chieftain. In an instant, he had seen the reasons for the Reach Antach's prosperity, and the inevitability of its destruction. This came together just as neatly. Although she was blind, the community chose not to identify her as such. If she sold a merit-chain for its silver value, she would be seen as the ruin of a fighting man. It would erode the goodwill on which she relied. Cete took the belt back from her. "I understand," he said.

"If you wish to commission an embroidery," she said, "use the belt to earn coin; I will make something fine for you."

"Thank you," he said. And he hesitated. The Reach

Antach had made an alliance that the city clans would have to destroy. It might be in a day, in a month, in ten years. But the Reach Antach would burn, and everyone who bore the name Antach would die. There was no reason for Cete to stay a moment longer than he had to, no reason to say his name within the walls of the Reach.

"I am Cete," he said.

"Marelle," she replied, and smiled. Her face showed the signs of long hours of hard work, rather than the untroubled smoothness of ease, and her hair was dark and coarse. She looked forward when she smiled, rather than to the side, and she showed her teeth, rather than merely turning up her lips. It was the smile of one man to another, rather than that of a woman to a man. But Cete could not help being struck by it.

"I will consider your advice, Marelle," said Cete, and with one last look at the embroidered sunset, he left.

He had arrived at Reach Antach an hour previous, looking for somewhere to stay. The town was a fine one, built on a strong position on a hilltop, with groves of olive and apricot down on the lower slopes. From all reports, the silver mines were profitable, and the soil was black, and smelled rich. The church was well built, with a scholar-priest of the Irimin school sitting on the dais, her mantle bound up with gold and silver threads that told of a great lineage and notable achievements. When Cete had gone in for the afternoon services, he had let himself hope that Reach Antach would suit. When the services were done, he knew that he would have to leave.

The cities built the reaches. They defended the walls as they went up, they provided dressed stone and cut lumber, they opened their storehouses until the reaches could feed themselves. In return, the reaches provided men and silver to the cities that had founded them, until the debt was paid. Repayment took centuries, and the reaches were always looking for quicker ways out. The method that the Reach Antach had chosen would never be allowed to succeed.

Cete knew he had to leave, but rather than taking him to the gate that would lead to Reach Tever, his feet brought him to the Brotherhood Hall, where men who had no clan connection would look to sell their labor, and those who needed labor would go to buy. Perhaps the crisis he had seen brewing would be delayed, or perhaps he could find work that would spare him from what he foresaw. But while it was far more likely to mean his death, he could not leave Reach Antach, could not walk away from the glory of that mantle or the hope of having something that fine for himself.

The Brotherhood Hall was not far from Marelle's shop, and its iron-bound doors were open. There were a half dozen older men inside, sipping cups of tea, chatting softly amongst themselves, and three times as many younger men standing in the artificially relaxed poses of men who felt they had something to prove. Exactly what one would expect from the Brotherhood Hall of a prosperous reach.

During the afternoon service, Cete had marked who had sat where. The man he had picked out as the factor of the mine—a thin man with little hair left and hands that showed no calluses—had sat among the scholars. Perhaps overly pious, but not excessively so, and unlikely to risk the smell of dealing badly. At least not in the open.

As Cete ambled towards him, the factor's eyes marked his merit chain, the fine-grained wood and thrice-forged steel of the axe Cete wore at his side, and the breadth of his shoulders. Not a fighting man, but a man who knew what to look for when evaluating warriors.

"Come in, be welcome," he said, standing. "Would you join us for tea?"

No contract.

If there were something to bargain for, the factor would have been less welcoming. "Thank you," said Cete. "It is a kind offer, for a stranger in your halls."

As was expected of him, he sat and drank tea for the better part of an hour. He talked with the older men, kept silent more often than speaking, showing his respect for their position and for their clan and for their Reach.

When enough time had passed, he finally broached the possibility of selling his labor. He had no expertise in pick or shovel, no apprenticeship in carpentry or fine metalwork, no training in the mathematics of pulley and lathe, of mine and trench. He had hoped that there would be some need for guards for the mines, or for the caravans carrying the silver back from the Reach to the city clans who owned the Antach debt, but at that suggestion, there was nothing but regretful shakes of the head.

"Full complement here," said the factor. "The tribes have been quiet of late, praise God, and the work has been steady; not many leave."

"I suppose the same is true of the private holders," said Cete. Most families had no need of protection beyond that which the clan armies and the troops of the Reach provided. But there were wealthy families who had reason to fear an enemy attack, and there were those who engaged in risky ventures, and there were those who pretended to the status of the one group or the other.

"Yes, and my apologies for saying so." The factor shook his head, an apologetic gesture. But there was nothing but pride in his eyes. "We are blessed in having veterans of the Reach army available for service, known to the heads of families and the private holders; there is little need to buy the work of outsiders, even from a man who wears a merit chain of the Hainst. Even the militia is at full complement." A militia contract was two days of labor a month, for training and drill—it wasn't enough to feed a man for a week. And not even that was available.

It all fit into place, all pointed to the same thing Cete had seen at the afternoon service. There was nothing unusual about a tribal chieftain attending services in a reach church during times of peace. The men of the tribes worshipped God with the same prayers as the men of the cities. But though one wore braids in his hair and beard, and a raw wool robe dyed red and blue, and the other had his hair closely cropped and wore the office chain of the head of a reach, there could be no mistaking the fact that chieftain and Antach were brothers. Of course the tribes had been quiet, of late. Of course peace had rippled out to the private holders. But when the ripples reached the cities, the wave would come crashing down upon them.

Well. Cete had made his choice; all that was left was to thank the mine factor for the tea, and get directions to the mustering grounds for the Reach army. No hope of winning a place in the Antach clan army, not without a connection. Besides, even if he could earn a place there, Cete would not take it. A remnant of the Reach army might survive the coming disaster. Of Clan Antach, there could be no survivors.

———————

The army of Reach Antach mustered outside the wall, below the northern gate. So far as Cete knew, there were no reaches north of Reach Antach, and certainly no cities. Just tribal lands, and wastes, and the endless stretch of the unknown; that there was a gate in the northern wall was a testament to hope; the army mustered beneath showed the sensible limits of those hopes.

The encampment didn't show any obvious rot. The clan and Reach banners were clean and crisp, there was no rust on the armor of the sentries, and the drills that Cete could see as he went down from the town towards the encampment were solid; footwork for long spear and training with axe and shield. There would be rot. If nothing else, Reach Antach had been enjoying an unnaturally extended period of peace and prosperity. But nothing could be seen on the surface.

The recruiting sergeant's tent flew the banners of Reach Antach, of Clan Antach, and of Clan Termith—a city clan. Cete tried to remember what he knew of the Antach's background. They'd been a family from the Coardur clan, and the Termith were one of the five city clans that had backed the Antach's claim to build a reach and become a clan themselves. Presumably, the Reach general was a Termith, and that's why their flag was flying. Cete went in, provoking a scowl from the sergeant behind the table, who had scattered skewers and lamb gristle amidst parchment scrolls.

"Fancy chain," said the sergeant. "How'd you get it?"

That wasn't necessarily a sign of rot; sergeants were not known for their manners.

"By performing a service for the Hainst chief," said Cete.

"Ha! Likely story. If you're in with the Hainst, what're you doing in the reaches?" There was a little gobbet of fat in the sergeant's beard. It bobbed when he talked, and Cete felt an urge to brush it off. Possibly with the head of an axe.

"The madding took a Hainst lordling in battle. I slew him. The service and exile came as one." It was a story that Cete preferred not to tell; his shoulders bowed with the weight of it. He ought to have anticipated. Eber Hainst was on the edge of madding often enough; Cete ought to have shifted his position so that he was not the one who had to kill Eber when the darkness swallowed him.

The recruiting sergeant shook his head, not quite dislodging the fat in his beard. "You never killed a warrior in the madding. Little guy like you, and old? More like it's a merit chain for rolling drunks in an alley."

If Cete fought this sergeant, he would be outlaw, win or lose. But when the time came, a reckoning would be paid.

The sergeant picked up a bit of bone and gristle, gnawed at it. "You want to list, you run the gauntlet."

"Fine," said Cete, his shoulders unlocking, his hands opening. There had been enough talk; it was time for blood. "Line it up." The gauntlet was more used as a threat or a punishment than as a recruiting test—men were injured regularly, maimed often. But he had set his purpose towards work in Reach Antach. Fighting was the work he knew, and this was the only buyer of the labor of fighting men in the Reach.

"Damn fool," said the sergeant. "Go on to field six, and wait there."

Whatever else this Reach army was, it was scarcely a welcoming place. For a moment, Cete considered turning around and leaving, taking his pack and heading on to Reach Tever or beyond, and leaving Antach to its fate.

But there was that mantle and the woman who had made it. Cete was a rational man, but the glory of her work had trapped him like a boar in a pit. He went to field six, folded his cloak and tunic atop his pack, laid his axe beside it, sat himself down on the earth, and prayed.

Cete did not count himself a pious man, but this was a time for prayer. He said the war psalms, lost himself in the poetry, bathed in the fire of the living God. When the gauntlet was assembled, he was ready. He knew what he would do.

Cete stood, stretched, smelled the dirt in the summer air, looked across the field. There were two lines of men drawn up, holding bludgeons and blunted swords. They were young, and their cotton arming shirts were a clean white, showing none of the ground-in rust that marked veterans. Too far apart for a proper gauntlet; they each wanted room to swing. They were almost all taller than him, and some were larger. Those he could see wore smiles, all broad white teeth. Cete held back his own smile.

There was a line drawn in the dirt between the two rows, and the sergeant was at the other end, all smiles as well. So many smiles; it was as though Sheavesday had come in summer. Cete could feel the blood pulsing in his neck, feel the shivering starting in his fingers. "Whenever you're ready, old man," said the sergeant.

"What are your rules?" asked Cete.

"Pretend to wear a merit chain, and you don't know the gauntlet?" laughed the sergeant. "Rule is this—walk the line from one end to the other. That's it. No other rules, no—"

Cete stepped forward. The first man on the left, holding an overseer's truncheon, moved first. He was tall and broadly built, with a child's face. The first man on the right was smaller, with pale, almost brown hair and a neatly cropped beard. He held a practice sword, and he pulled it back to strike.

Cete grabbed the man with the truncheon by his elbow, pushing in close while the weapon was still raised, and punched him in the center of his chest at the same time, moving with all his weight. The man showed more surprise than pain at that, the sort of stupefied, half-embarrassed look that Cete had seen on countless faces of men who had taken a mortal blow in battle.

The sword was coming down. Cete pivoted, sent the big man into the man with the cropped beard. Cropped beard fell back, as did the man next to him, who'd gotten tangled in his fellow soldier's elbows. If Cete had let go of the big man, all three of them would've been off the line until he was past. He didn't. One hand on the elbow, the other on the wrist, and he twisted. The boy dropped to a knee. Cete let go of the elbow and drove a fist into his nose. The crunch of cartilage and blood, the tears of pain. Another punch, this one in his eye. That rocked his head back; the boy had enough muscle in his neck that it wasn't a killing blow, but he was unquestionably out.

One last punch. Cheekbone, just under the eye. No

point in that but showing the others what would happen to them. The head rocked back again. This time, Cete let the boy fall, pulling the truncheon loose from nerveless fingers.

The smiles were gone.

The young soldiers looked white around the edges, nauseated, afraid. Eighteen of them—seventeen, now— and one of him. Cete gave a battle roar, full-throated, from his core, and they took a step back. He walked forward, truncheon swinging loosely, and they blanched. They'd get their courage back, and there were too many of them, too young, for him to beat them all. But at least they knew that staying on the line meant a blooding.

Before he could get to them, the sergeant came roaring through. "I'll see you bled for this, you outclan swine!" There was spittle on his beard and wildness in his eyes. Cete felt his muscles tense, felt the length of the truncheon in his hand. Could be that he would bleed for it, but he couldn't help what he was about to do, any more than he could leave the mantle behind. It was the edge of the madding; it was his rage, not his mind, which would swing the truncheon.

"A three-year veteran, and you a grayhair trash!" shouted the sergeant. Just another step, two, and Cete would have the range on him. He could already hear the crack of wood on skull, feel the shock going up his arm.

The madding had not quite swallowed him, but it was getting close.

"Attention!" came a shout from outside the field, and the sergeant stopped. Another step, another half a step, and Cete would've started his swing, would've killed or been killed.

"Sir!" said the sergeant.

"What's this?" asked another voice, not shouting, but with a clear note of command. All eyes had turned to the interloper, but no pause had been called for the gauntlet. Cete could push past, he could step up and crack the sergeant's skull open. He did neither, but nor did he turn away to see the man who was talking. Cete was balanced on the point of a knife.

"This outclan grayhair heard there was easy meat for no work here, sir, so he faked up some story with a merit chain. Then he cheated at the gauntlet, hurt young Arthran bad, sir. Nothing to concern you, sir; I'll deal with it."

A laugh. "You'll get your fool head cracked open, Sergeant Mase. Arthran's half his age and has a foot of height on him, and he's a damn bloody pulp. Didn't you hear that battle roar?"

The sergeant hesitated, took a half step forward, hesitated. Cete crouched, ready, willing himself back from the edge.

"Enough." The man who had been talking vaulted the fence into the exercise yard, the smooth leap of a young man secure in his strength. All the soldiers stood at attention, including the sergeant and, after a breath, Cete. "You wear a merit chain of the Hainst."

"Yes," said Cete.

"Have you held command before?"

Cete hesitated. Before he had been cast from the Hainst, he had been a captain general; he had left that behind, and had not allowed himself to want it since. "Yes," he said.

"I am Radan Termith; I am captain general here. How are you called?" Radan wore a commander's armor, lacquered scale and inlaid plate, and he wore it well. Long hair, black and thick, and a close-cropped beard. Young, nearly as young as the soldier who Cete had laid out, but he wasn't showing arrogance or deference, just the easy assurance of command.

"I am Cete." Sergeant Mase ground his teeth at that, but Cete had no reason to defer to the commander; he was not under orders.

"Well, Cete," said Radan. "You're looking for work?"

"I am," said Cete.

"I will buy from you three years of work as a fifty-commander, at the rate of one half-mark a day, one quarter paid in advance, one quarter on completion, and the rest every tenth day of service."

Cete had been hoping for a short-term contract, something he could walk clear of if he saw the hammer start to fall. He'd hoped to temporize, rather than commit; it had been foolish.

"These terms are acceptable to me," he said. "My labor is yours for the term you have specified, sir."

Radan leapt back over the fence, where a half-dozen junior officers waited. "The contracts will be drawn up, and your first payment prepared. Report to the quartermaster after the evening services; he will have your contract, your initial payment, and your assignment."

Radan gave the exercise yard one last look. "See to Arthran, Mase," he said. "And be less of a fool, if that's at all possible."

"Yes, sir," said Mase, and knelt beside the man whose truncheon Cete still held. A fifty-commander was a lieutenant-captain, and it was no longer appropriate for Cete to bear a grudge against a sergeant who was to serve alongside him. Which did not mean that there was no longer a reckoning due.

Cete dropped the truncheon and walked to the end of the line. The rest of the soldiers were no longer on the gauntlet, but if he left it undone, it would mean one thing, and finishing it meant another. Then he left the yard, headed back towards the Reach. It was not a wise decision, but it was made. He was a fifty-commander in the army of Reach Antach, sworn to the Antach of the Antach, and to his commander, Radan Termith. Their doom was his. Now he would see what that decision had gained him.

———————

There was more of Marelle's work hanging from the walls within her shop. A woman's festival gown, with irises and orchids twined on the sleeves, a prayer mantle with broad stripes of geometric patterns, clothing embroidered with flowers and constellations, hawks and hounds, bold patterns and subtle. Nothing there could match the sunset mantle, but all of it was beautiful.

"I should like to commission from you a mantle," he said. Marelle was sitting in a straight-backed chair, her fingers pulling a red thread through a white cloth as she stared off into the middle distance.

"How much?" she asked.

Cete considered. He would have a hundred and fifty marks as his first payment. As an officer, he would have to pay for lodgings, he'd need some money set aside to cover gaps in issued equipment and pay for festival meals for his command. The most he could spare was twenty marks from the initial payment, and then two of the five he'd receive every ten days. Fifty, if he could wait until the Sheavesday festival. Fifty marks could buy a man a house, or ten olive trees, or twenty-one sheep.

"Sixty," he said, "I will give you twenty tomorrow, and the rest on delivery."

"I will trust you to pay for what you purchase," she said, drawing back slightly, the faintest hint of offense in her voice.

"I am now a fifty-commander in the Reach army," said Cete. "And I have no friends or relations within two month's travel." Or within ten year's travel, but that was of less concern to the law. "If I die, all I own will be given to charity. I do not want you to work for me and receive nothing."

"Most men think that the Reach army is a safe, if dull occupation," said Marelle.

"They are wrong," said Cete.

Marelle nodded. He was an outsider, and she would have heard that the Reach army was safe from men who had lived in the Reach for decades, but she didn't show any signs of surprise or disbelief at his pronouncement. "You think that war is coming?" she asked.

"When I went to the church for the afternoon service," said Cete, "the Antach of Antach was there, at the dais. Next to him sat a man with the victory braids of a tribal chief in his hair and beard."

"Tribesmen fear God as well as we do," said Marelle. "If they come in peace, their chiefs are accorded all honor—that's mere prudence."

"Yes," said Cete. "But for all their differences—the Antach in his city mantle, the tribesman in his robes— there could be no mistaking the fact that the men were brothers."

Marelle's lips quirked up in a smile. "It is supposed to be the deepest-held secret of the Reach," she said.

Cete forbore mentioning that if a blind woman could see it, it could not be such a great secret as all that. "Then they ought never have been seen together. I cannot say how it was arranged, but the city clans cannot allow it. The enmity of the tribes is the leash around the neck of the Reaches. It extends their debts from years to centuries, forces them to rely on the arms of the city, to pay double for everything. If one reach slips its lead, the others will follow. A war is coming, and I do not think that the Antach will be permitted to win."

"The Antach thinks," started Marelle, and then shrugged. "But I think that he is wrong, and that you are right." She stopped her embroidering, a length of scarlet thread between her hand and the white fabric. "If you joined the Reach army on my urging, I am sorry for it."

"You spoke only good sense," said Cete. "I will have the money for you tomorrow."

"I will make something fine for you," said Marelle. "Before Sheavesday."

With that done, Cete felt almost giddy. That it was commissioned did not mean it would ever be completed. Death came to all men; he might never see it done, even if it were finished. But he had made his choice, and now he had made his commission.

"How comes it that a clan lord has a brother who is chief of a clan?" he asked. There had not previously been space in his mind for that question.

"In the clans, descent is through the father," said Marelle. "In the tribes, the mother. The father of the Antach took two wives. With their knowledge and consent—they were both ambitious women."

Within the law, but outside of custom. Ambitious, certainly, but foolish just as surely. They talked for a time about that, and about other things, until it was almost time for the evening services, and Cete had to make his hurried farewells. It was only later that he realized he had not spoken to Marelle about his commission, had not specified what colors he wanted, or what pattern. Well and good; he could not have imagined that sunset sky, clouded with birds. He had no doubt that Marelle's eyes could not see, and he had no doubt that he lacked her vision.

Chapter 2

The payment and the orders were ready after the evening services, as Radan had said, and Cete spent most of the night reviewing the contract. There was seldom much difference in the arrangements offered to outclan fighting men, but it was only good sense to read through what had been given to him to sign. His life and his obligations to God were bound up in those parchments, so it was well to be certain of those chains.

As he suspected, most of the weight was on his shoulders. He had no clan to guarantee him, or to protect him in case of default or misconduct by his captain general or the Antach of the Antach. The only protections he had were those the law gave to any fighting man, and his only guarantor was the Lord God. If he was slain unlawfully, no clan had the right of feud with the Antach, and if the Antach wished, his contract could be ended at any time, under any circumstances, with only payment in money to soothe his wounded honor.

There was a time when the Hainst would have stood behind him, and if he signed with another clan, his rights would have had a guardian. But that time was long gone, and better forgotten. Cete signed, and claimed his silver. Early the next morning, he met his fifty on the practice yards.

As with all Reach armies, they went through the dawn routine with sword and axe before the morning services. Watching that routine, Cete saw the work that he would have to do. It was not a bad command. He had fought alongside worse, stood shoulder to shoulder with raw recruits, with criminals, with garrison troops accustomed to wine and ease. There were some of those there, but the bulk of his fifty were sober fighting men, men who had learned their routines as youths and had practiced them faithfully as adults.

The problem was that there were too many outclan, from too many clans, and the difference in routines was painfully obvious. There were men accustomed to the wall-walk where Cete expected locked arms, or who dipped, turned, and reached where he thought the dawn routine should show straight cuts. Men bumped each other, fell out of time, swore.

Radan Termith had given him a command, but it was a command of men like Cete, rather than a command of children of the Reach. Fair enough—the politics of the Reach clans could be poisonous, and he had been given a post that ought to have gone to a Reach army veteran—

but it was scarcely a soft posting. Fair enough, as well. The Reach general had shown faith in Cete's word and in his skill, and Cete would reward that faith tenfold.

It was not just the dawn routine that was the problem; it was the attitudes that drove the form, the assumptions that the fighting traditions made about attack and counter, how the others in ranks would strike, what would be considered an opening, and what would drive men back to defensive poses. If he could count on some months free, Cete would have started them from the beginning, either with the tradition in which he was raised, or in the traditions of the Reach Antach. But the crisis could come any day, and if his men met it halfway between traditions, it would be a disaster.

The best he could do was to redivide the squads. There were too many traditions for that to work neatly, but there were enough similarities and differences that he could find patterns. It was ugly and inefficient, and would never produce the perfect uniformity of routine that distinguished a superior command. But it would work in the field, and Cete could think of nothing else that would.

The differences limited him, but within those limits, Cete pushed as hard as a man could. Days stretched into weeks as Cete pounded his men into shape. It was a good deal more than the other commands went through, and naturally, the men resented it. Which meant that more of

Cete's money went towards festive meals and donatives, and that more of Cete's blood and time went into the exercise yards.

All of his funds that were left over and much of his time went to Marelle and his commission. He never asked what she was making, and she never broached the subject. There were other things that they did not discuss—Marelle's blindness, how long it would be before the city clans ended the Reach Antach, why Cete had chosen to stay instead of leaving for a less perilous reach. And yet, somehow, they found enough to say to each other, or shared their silences in her shop, or on the porch of Cete's shabby little house.

When an unmarried man spent so much of his time with an unmarried woman, it excited rumors. Cete ignored them, and Marelle made no mention of having heard anything untoward. If Cete had any expectation of surviving the years for which he had sold his labor, he might have put forward a suit, but as it was, there was no point in thinking in those terms. When the time came, he would earn his thing of beauty with his death. Until then, he would forget it as best he could, sitting in Marelle's shop and talking with her of other things.

The waiting ended just over a month after Cete found his place in the Reach army. The day after the fast of the Summer Candles, the Antach of the Antach had the

Reach army muster up beneath the walls, and blessed them as they marched out, headed north. Only the wall fifty, the militia, and the Antach clan army were held in reserve; the rest followed Radan, banners held high. The tribes would be in their deepest summer grazing lands, far from the reaches, and since the summer sheaves were not in, it'd be a strain on the Reach to support an army in the field. It was not a propitious time for a raid.

They struck out on pilgrim roads and dry riverbeds, marching so fast that the scouts and slingers who took to the hilltops were barely able to keep pace with them. Risky. It was good country for an ambush, with long fields of grazing land between steep and wooded hills. No chance that a local tribe would miss them, and the column would do poorly if the tribesmen chose the place to give battle.

So. Out into tribal lands, out of season, with no fear of local tribesmen. The assumption had to be that a foreign clan had come into the lands claimed by the Antach's brother, and posed a threat to the Reach. It seemed the city clans had made a move, and that the Antach—the Antach and his general—had learned of it early enough that they were trying to preempt the tribal attack, hit them before they could come within sight of Reach Antach.

For the first time since Cete had taken Radan's commission, he let himself feel hope. If the Antach had an ally among the city clans who gave them information on the coming attack, and if the Antach were close enough to the local tribes that they could march their army out with impunity, perhaps Reach Antach would be able to throw off the leash of the city clans. If they could, the rewards . . .

Cete didn't let himself dwell on that possibility. There was a river of blood between the Reach Antach and security, and he had taken silver to wade through that river. His concern was not what lay on that further shore, or even how best to reach it. His job was to find a way not to drown, within the limits of the law, and his duties, and his honor.

The Reach army was moving too fast to properly fortify each night. There were pickets up, and quickly raised barricades of branch and thorn, but they only stopped marching when it was already too dark to dig proper lines.

The enemy they sought found them on the fourth morning out of Reach Antach, just as they were breaking their camp. It had been a risky site, but they'd been moving too fast to make good camps. That night, it had been a stretch of land cropped clear by sheep, spread out across both sides of a dry riverbed. The tribesmen had crept up through a copse of bottomland oak and terebinth trees, and burst from cover with the whistle of javelin and the wavering, terrifying battle yell of the northwestern tribes.

Cete and his fifty were on the same side of the streambed as the tribesmen, and his men, at least, were in harness, with weapons ready. No time to find the signal-man; he'd have to command by action. He ran, axe loose and warm in his grip, legs eating the ground, finding his footing without thought. First ten-squad came in behind him, third and fourth formed up for the charge.

They passed a bloodied sentry, hit a tribesman who had gotten in front of the rest and cast him aside, the whole fifty iron-hungry, despite the whistle and tramp of an oncoming foe. Then, behind them, the signal horns blew the retreat.

Another moment on the point of a knife. Orders were to be followed, and they were not yet at grips. Law and custom were as clear on that as anything. But they were the wrong damn orders. Try to get back across that streambed, and they'd be clawing at the bank like stranded turtles while the tribesmen skewered them from behind. It might have made sense to Radan—the bed would make a fine ditch between them and the tribes—but the tribesmen would blood them and fade away, and they were three days from the Reach.

The horns blew again. Cete shook his head, and charged on, and his men followed. Even if he was violating the chain of command, they, at least, knew to obey it. His sin was not theirs. Three more heartbeats, and they were in among the tribesmen, and no law or custom allowed a commander to call off a troop once they had come to grips.

If nothing else, he'd secured a retreat for those with better discipline. Then all thoughts of strategy, all thoughts of right and wrong vanished, and there was nothing but sword and axe and knife and blood, the push of line against line.

The first wave of tribesmen went down. They had courage, but lacked the discipline of the cities—each tribesman fought to prove himself, to win acclaim and honor, but Cete's troops fought because that was what they had learned, because they had been trained to do nothing other than fight when the blood began to flow.

First wave down, second wave coming. Not the heroes of the first line, not young men trying to prove themselves, but the fighting men of a northern tribe, beards and hair tied back, mail shirts and brass embossed shields. Man for man, the Reach army was their better, but there were too many of them. Step by step by step, Cete and his men were forced back to the riverbank. Before them, a mass of fighting men, hundreds of tribal warriors, with goat-skin standards and red-painted shields. Behind them, a drop almost as tall as a man, and bleached stones beneath.

Damn Radan! The boy had looked fine, and they had been right to march out to meet this threat, but if he was to be a field general, he had to see that circumstances had changed. Now was the time to call for the slingers and ladders, now was the time for a counterattack. The surprise was gone, and Cete had a beachhead for him. Cete had disobeyed, but he had been right, and Radan had to take the advantage that Cete's fifty had earned.

It had not just been his fifty who had remained on the weak side of the streambed. Others had not heard the call to retreat, or had come to grips before it was blown, or had not chosen to obey. But there were less than eighty of the Reach men, and they were falling fast. Cete ducked underneath a spear, which skidded across his shoulder. He pushed up, axe in one hand, knife in the other, and found the weak point in his opponent's mail shirt. The knife cut in at the armpit, and the tribesman pulled back, howling in pain.

Two more came in, and went down, but all along the riverbank his men were dying. Three patches held. Where he stood was the first squad, and remnants of the fourth; he could not tell who was left alive. He could hear the soft sounds of a ready army behind him, amidst all the thunder and shouting of the melee. If Cete had kept his horn, he'd have blown the charge himself, and to hell with the consequence, but that was long gone, trampled with his tent or taken as a trophy.

There was a pause in the assault, just an instant, and Cete looked back over the dry riverbed. There was Radan, his face white beneath his helmet, horn to hand. He was young enough that this might have been his first real battle.

Cete took a spear in the center of his chest. It dropped him to one knee, but it didn't cut his armor, or knock him back into the streambed. The roar came up from inside him, forced out from his chest, loud enough to hurt his throat. He was on his feet, his foe was gone, and he was holding a fistful of hair. He had no recollection of what had happened; his vision was going white around the edges, and while his fingers still gripped his weapons, he could no longer feel them. The edge and the breath of the madding.

He leapt forward, beyond the knot of his men, into the face of his enemies. Cete had always known how he would die.

Behind him, as though through a very long tunnel, the trumpets blew the charge. A hook-bladed knife gashed into the side of his face; his axe took off the hand that held it, so the spray of the tribesman's blood met his own in midair. Another spear in the center of his chest, as he moved through the blood. This one caught between two plates in his armor, and the man behind it tried to push through the chain and arming shirt. Cete's axe came up and around, cut the spearpoint off just beyond the tang. He was pushed forward, forward by the weight of the men behind him.

Cete staggered, held his ground, did his best to distinguish between the tribesmen and the Reach army. They started singing the war hymn, which helped. He joined in the chorus, found his voice in theirs, found his center in the tramp of armored men moving as one. The tribesmen had been pushing his fifty-command hard, but against the force of the Reach army, they were the ones who fell, they were the ones who turned to flee.

Then the terrain the tribesmen had chosen worked against them. It was too broken, too steep for easy flight. Warriors tripped over roots, caught their feet in brambles, fell and were killed by spear and axe. The trumpets blew the halt as the tribal army thinned out, fled in too many directions to follow as a troop. This time, that caution was correct. It did not seem likely to Cete that the tribes were trying to lead them into an ambush, but he had seen too often their courage; they were fleeing because they were losing. As soon as the odds evened, they would turn and fight, ferocious as boars at bay.

Cete could not remember where he had left his dagger—in a tribesman's belly, perhaps, or knocked from his grip and trampled into the gory earth—but there was no shortage of replacements. He picked up a hook-bladed tribal knife and stuck it in his belt. It was longer than the dagger that the Reach army had issued, and the balance was different, but it was a fine tool. It would serve.

More than two hundred men of the tribes lay on the field made muddy with their gore, their weapons taken as trophies or heaped up and burned. Of the Reach army, no more than thirty men had fallen, twenty-three of whom were from Cete's fifty. Eight others had taken serious wounds, three of whom were unlikely to survive to see the Reach Antach again. Cete walked at the head of a sadly diminished line, but a proud one; the victory was theirs, and they knew it.

Already, the ravens were settling on the branches of the oaks and terebinths, croaking at one another and watching the men beneath with first one eye, and then the other. Already, broad winged vultures circled, drifting without the slightest motion of wing or tail. Soon, the Reach army would leave, taking their spoils and their slain with them, and the ravens and vultures would have their share. It would be a long time before the tribesmen returned to that field, split through by a dry riverbed.

The army spent two more days marching outward, but the tribesmen did not show themselves a second time, and the supply pouches from the Reach grew thin.

They reached a hilltop, raised up there a prayer altar, and offered their psalms of praise, and begged forgiveness for their transgressions. Then they turned back for the Reach, scouts and slingers ranging on the hills beside the column, waiting for the tribesmen to avenge their slain.

Chapter 3

Six days later, they returned to the walls of the Reach Antach. There had been no further ambush or attack, no
trace of tribesmen, hostile or friendly. It had been as fine
a raid as any Cete had ever seen. More than two hundred tribesmen dead, dozens more likely to die of their
wounds, and a great wealth in arms and armor taken
or destroyed. The strike by the Reach would have been
death for most tribes, their standards left to rot as the survivors begged to share the tents of cousins and second
cousins. Nothing less than a confederation of tribes
would be able to raid again for a generation. And they
had only lost forty men of the Reach—thirty in the fighting, and ten more of their wounds. For all that included
twenty-eight men of Cete's fifty, he did not count himself
disappointed with his performance in the field, and his
surviving soldiers held their heads high.

It seemed that the other commanders did not fault
him for his losses. After spending the ritual night outside
the walls, after the army was purified by the priests, they
marched back through the northern gate of Reach An-

tach. As they came up to the gate, two other commanders came up behind Cete and lifted him up on their shoulders.

They sang the battle hymn as they carried him through the gate, and Cete was amazed to feel tears on his face. During the weeks of training, the other commanders had not said much to him, good or ill, and both he and his troop had known themselves to be outclan. They had sold their labor to fight for the Reach Antach, but they were not of it. Now, it seemed that those who lived were men of the Reach Antach. As he was carried back into the Reach, Cete felt a part of him that had died when he left Hainst the City coming back to life.

Once he was through the gate, they let him down, clapped him on the shoulder, and then they all sang the battle hymn together as they marched on towards the church. All along the streets, women and children and laboring men watched. Some were cheering from the moment the Reach army returned singing. Others watched with anxious eyes until they caught sight of the face they sought, and only then did they join in the general celebration. It was thanks to Cete's fifty that there were not more who turned away shaking and pale, or who joined the procession behind the linen-wrapped stretchers, crying silently in the smell of the cypress branches and saxifrage.

The joy that they had felt coming through the gate diminished when they reached the courtyard of the church. Radan Termith was there, as was the Antach of the Antach, and Lemist Irimin, scholar-priest of Reach Antach. They were all wearing the white mantles that men wore to atone, or for their burials, or for when they sat in judgment.

There was the pale limestone facing of the church behind them, and the long gray wall that marked the limits of sanctified land all around. Soon all the congregation of the Reach stood in the courtyard, men and women, soldiers and stonemasons. The sweat cooled on Cete's back as the battle-hymn quieted and was still. The men who had marched out to fight the tribes walked hesitantly into the church courtyard, to hear why Captain General Termith had raced ahead of his army into the Reach, and why he had called the Antach and the priest to sit with him in judgment, in front of the whole congregation.

"What is the law," said Radan, when there was at last silence, "when a fifty-commander disregards the order to withdraw, and causes the death of half of his command by his refusal to obey orders?"

The world tilted, circled around; Cete tried to keep from falling down.

"The law is that the forehead of this fifty-commander should be cut open so that his scar shall always be seen, his back should be lashed seventy times with a rod of myrtle or with a whip of calf-skin, and he should dwell on the outside of the camp," said Lemist, slowly. She was old, and when she led the services, or delivered a sermon, she would speak carefully, not letting her words run away with her. But she was not this slow. She saw what was being done, and did not approve.

Nor did the Antach of the Antach look pleased to be sitting in judgment, trailing the skirts of his white mantle in the dirt of the church courtyard. The chairs they had brought out were fine work; cedar and cypress and sycamore, but none of them looked entirely comfortable in them; Lemist and the Antach were uneasy, and Radan . . . Radan was risking a great deal, and Cete did not know why. Radan called witness after witness to stand before the leaders of the community and the whole congregation. Each told what they had seen; there were no falsehood spoken before that tribunal. Some of the witnesses—his men, the other generals, men who had lived when they would have died—tried to explain why Cete had been right. As Radan cut them off, and called others to confirm what had happened on the field, Cete did his best to think through what was happening, and why.

The letter of the law was against him, and he had no clan that would demand mercy, no patron with standing to argue that Radan's orders had been criminally flawed. That he knew as soon as the accusation was made. It did not take long for all those gathered to know it as well, as all the details were drawn out through witnesses, through questions to the priest and to the Antach, through consultation of the law.

"And now," said Radan, when the witnesses were done, when Cete could find no point of law to justify his disobedience, when the sun was low enough in the sky for the afternoon service to begin, "unless the lord of the Reach chooses to override my judgment and authority, I shall adjust the verdict through my right as captain, and administer justice."

There. That was it. It finally all fit into place. The tribe that had been raised up against the Reach was not the only arrow in the quiver of the city clans. They had another, far deadlier bolt, and Cete could at last see it, just before it sank into his breast.

Radan Termith, captain general of the army of Reach Antach, was committed to the destruction of the Reach Antach, and of the Antach clan. That was why he had camped recklessly, that was why he had blown the retreat, and that was why he had waited so long before sounding the charge. He needed the trust of the people of the Reach to see his task through, and he had given up much of that trust by prosecuting Cete, and at long last,

Cete understood why.

He could see it on the face of the Antach. Whether or not he overrode his general to grant clemency to the fifty-commander who had saved his army, he would lose. If he let the trial take its course, Radan would grant clemency himself. The Antach would lose the trust of his men, and Radan would gain it. That would mean their deaths at the hands of the next tribe the city clans raised, and his own soon after.

If he overrode Radan, Radan would lose the respect of the troops, and the Antach would be seen as a protector of his men; well and good, but it would also lay the grounds for breaking the contract between Radan Termith and the Reach Antach. Unlike Cete's contract, which rested on the bare bedrock of the law, Radan's contract would have teeth to it. There would be financial protection, and there would be the honor of the Termith staked . . . it would have been structured to give the Termith grounds for feud if the contract was broken. The Antach could not second-guess his general, not without giving the armies of Clan Termith grounds to set out from Termith the City, with law and custom marching alongside.

Either way, if Cete would remain silent, either Radan or the Antach would pardon him, and he'd see it through with his scars all honorable scars, and with his position intact. If he played it right, he could stand at Radan's shoulder, and when the axe fell on the Reach Antach, there might be a home for him in Termith.

As the accused, Cete had been sitting on the ground, before the tribunal. Now he stood, back straight, head held high. "I ask no mercy," said Cete. "I claim no clemency from man. The captain general has chosen to prosecute me for my violations of the laws of battle. Let the sentence be carried out, so that the law shall not be broken."

The priest looked troubled, the general looked furious, and the Antach looked like a man reprieved from the gallows. Cete locked eyes with him, the man who was his lord, and for whom he had chosen to be branded as an outcast, to be whipped and beaten. "Lay on, then!" said Cete, his voice loud in the silence. "Or have you assembled this congregation for nothing?"

Next to the Antach, Radan seethed. This was not what he had intended. He had given up a great deal, and gained nothing by it. The most expendable of his fifty-commanders, the man chosen to be his winning stone, had walked off the board and made him look a fool. "Then let it be carried out, if that is your wish," said Radan, the smoothness gone from his voice and manner. "Sergeant Mase! Execute the sentence of the court and of the whole congregation."

Mase stepped forward out of the ranks, took the myrtle rod from the hand of the priest, its bark as dark as skin, the knife from the belt of the Antach, its blade as clear as dawn. Radan leaned forward as Mase stepped past, gave him his instructions too quietly for Cete to hear. Mase looked troubled at those words, lost the spring in his step that he had on being called forward.

As Mase went through the preparations for the scarring and the lashes, removing Cete's shirt and laying it to the side, binding Cete's arms in front of him, and getting a blessing from the priest and from the Antach, Cete considered what Radan might have said. He had outplayed the captain general, but Radan would still be looking for an escape. Then Mase came forward with the knife, and thought fled.

Mase cut open Cete's forehead, pulled back a flap of skin, so the blood flowed down freely.

This was it; this was the end. There was no Reach so remote, no city clan so desperate to take on a fighting man with that scar. If he wished to work with his axe again, he could perhaps become a bandit in the hillcountry—even the tribes would know what that mark meant, and even they would not have him.

Cete did not allow himself to weep, but the blood dripped down like tears.

Mase then took his stance a step and a half behind

Cete. "Knew you'd come to a bad end," he said, and Cete felt his old grudge against Mase rising up in his breast. Of course. That was it; yet another scheme from the captain general.

Radan had seen what had passed between Cete and Mase. He did not want Cete as a living reminder of what he had done, begging at the outskirts of the Reach, so he had told Mase to kill him with the rod. The men would think it was part of the grudge between Cete and the sergeant, and some of the stain of what had happened would leave Radan's hands, to fall on Mase, who would be sacrificed at some later point, to win back a measure of respect from the men.

The words that Mase had said about his honor chain still lay between them, but this was more important. "Strike as you have been ordered, Sergeant Mase," said Cete, loud enough to be heard by the assembled congregation. "I know that it is not your hand moving the rod." He looked across at Radan Termith, and saw the hatred blaze up there. He had been right, and now that stain would not spread. Radan had destroyed him, but he would not escape any of the blame for that destruction.

If the man with the whip or rod killed a man who was being lashed, he was liable for a charge of murder. Perhaps Radan would push that through, have Mase executed as well. Cete had said what he had said, so if Radan did that, he'd be murdered in the street. While that would give ample grounds for the Termith to declare a feud with the Antach, Cete did not think their son would chose that method of seeing their aim accomplished. Mase would live, and Radan would be hated.

The first blow struck high across the shoulders, with all the force that Mase could bring to bear. Cete stood, breathing hard. It hurt, but he had been hurt before. There was worse to come. The second hit the same spot, exactly. This one was harder to ignore. The third was worse, as was the fourth. After that, Cete stopped counting, fought to keep on his feet, fought to keep his screams from escaping, fought to keep from showing his fear and his agony.

The intent of flogging was not death, but in the hands of a strong man, the myrtle rod could kill—had killed, would kill, was killing Cete. He had always known that he would die by violence, but he had never thought it would hurt so much—the sudden pain of being opened by an axe, the desperate choking of strangulation or a cut throat, the vomiting agonies of a stomach wound—not the steady gashing of a myrtle wand, not with the eyes of the populace upon him, not with that scar on his forehead.

Another blow, and another, and another. All upon his shoulders, as the law demanded. His skin had been broken early on; they were cutting into meat—he was being sawed apart, stroke by stroke, and he had to stand and take it, his blood watering the dirt of the church's courtyard. He looked across at Radan, and the captain general looked back, the ice in Radan's eyes a match for the fire across Cete's shoulders. He had chosen his enemy, and he had not chosen a man who lacked the stomach to see bloody work done.

Another blow, no harder than the others had been, but no softer either. This one knocked him down to his knees. Was it twenty? Thirty? It didn't matter; he wouldn't live to see seventy. Cete struggled back to his feet, and the next blow knocked him down again. A third time, and he didn't try to rise.

Mase brought the rod down, and Cete coughed at the impact, blood spatting from his mouth. The pain was overwhelming, but it was less, somehow. Another blow, and it all seemed strangely distant. It was strange—if he had let the Antach choose mercy or disgrace, he would now be in the church, secure in the affections of the army, and warm. Another blow, which he scarcely felt at all.

And then something was draped over his shoulders that was not a myrtle rod. It was soft, everywhere except where the rod had been striking, where it burned like fire. "Stand away, woman," shouted Mase.

Cete struggled. He could not rise, but he pushed his

weight up to his elbows, tried to turn around. "And if the man who has been judged guilty cannot stand before his blows," said Marelle, quoting the law, "let him go out with a partial count, for there is on him no judgment of death."

"He'll take what I have for him," said Mase. "It's my decision—"

If it was Marelle . . . Cete saw what had been thrown over his shoulders, and tried to shake it off. It was the sunset mantle, and he was bleeding into it. All else that had passed—his placement on the riverbank, the fight, the trial, all of it—it might not have been just, but it had all fit; it had all been part of a logical pattern. Blood on the mantle was wrong, wronger than his scarring, wronger than what Mase and Radan were doing.

"A blind woman thinks she can see better than a soldier in arms!" shouted Radan, coming up from his seat for the first time, shaking in rage. Perhaps it did fit; Cete's blood on Radan's mantle, his stain on the glory that the general had commissioned. Still, he could not bear to see the mantle damaged; Cete struggled to take it off, but could not.

"A blind woman can hear," said Marelle. "But a soldier in arms sees what he is ordered to see!"

The crowd had been silent, utterly silent since the verdict had been passed. Now murmurs were starting. "Go, then," said Radan. "And take the rag with you. You shall not receive good silver for stained and damaged goods."

At that insult, something within Cete broke. There was law, and there was policy, and there was the fate of Reach Antach—they all said that he had to leave Radan be. But if he could have stood, he would have killed him. He tried, rose up to his knees, and fell again, his hands reaching for the axe he was not wearing. This was the madding, the true madding, but his body was too weak to hold it. Cete fell forward from his knees, back down, and all he knew as darkness took him was that Marelle was at his side.

Chapter 4

Cete woke in pain. He was lying on his stomach, and his shoulders burned where he had been struck. There was blood on the sheets beneath him, blood on his pillow from the cut in his forehead. That had not hurt until he remembered it. When he did, it hurt far worse than his back.

His next thought was of Marelle. She had saved his life, what was left of it. She had saved his life, but the general of the Reach had called her blind in the face of the congregation, and she had admitted it. She had saved the life of an outcast, at the cost of being cast out herself.

By the light coming in through the window, the sun was setting, but it was not yet down. Cete pulled himself from the bed, wincing at the pain in his back, at the sticky flow of blood where wounds pulled back open. The room tilted and swirled around him as he stood. He nearly fell as he took one step, another.

He gritted his teeth against the pain. The door was four steps away; if he had a cane, he could have managed it. He fell, down to one knee, struggled back up. Three

59

more steps. Two.

"You can't," said Marelle, from somewhere behind him. He hadn't seen her when he first saw the mantle. He hadn't seen her amidst the congregation at the courtyard of the church, he hadn't seen her in her house. She was blind, and he could see, but somehow she always seemed to be close to him, without him realizing.

"Have to," grunted back Cete. "Not married. Can't have you prosecuted as a whore."

"He wouldn't," said Marelle. "Radan Termith is no fool. If he pushes too hard, he'll be stoned in the street, and the people of the Reach will leave to join the tribes. It's not what the Termith want, and it's not what he wants."

"Not him," said Cete, staggering forward, getting hold of the doorpost. "A hanger-on. Someone who thinks it'd make Radan happy."

Outside, he could see more of the house he had been in. It wasn't Marelle's house in the city; the blind, those suffering from cholera or leprosy, and all others who were cast out of the congregation had to live outside the walls. But it was a fine stone house, with a broad-timbered roof, and an orchard.

The orchard fence was a high one; more than shoulder high on a man, which meant that it would count as inside her house in the eyes of the law. Cete pulled himself up to standing. Marelle came out of the door behind him, tucked herself in under his arm, taking some of his weight, giving him balance.

"It's unlikely," she said, as they walked towards the fence's gate.

"You'll not suffer more on my account," said Cete.

Marelle gave a snort at that. "Also unlikely," she replied, but said nothing else until Cete was beyond the gate, with the sun still above the western hills.

"You'll wait here?" she asked, and Cete nodded.

Marelle returned to her house, came back with blankets and a stone jug filled with water, and left them with Cete. "It's as safe a house as there is, beyond the wall," she said, "and my neighbors will watch over you until I return. You'll stay here?"

Cete wanted to ask where she was going, what they could do, but the walk had emptied him out. He nodded, made no argument as she draped a blanket over him, and watched as she strode away, her steps confident and her back straight.

His back hurt too much for him to fall completely asleep, but Cete drifted in and out of consciousness. It had been a hot day, but the cold came on with the sunset, so he appreciated the blanket. The sunset was a fine one, all pinks and reds, and the nightjars and bats came out of the shadows to hawk at moths and mosquitoes.

There were two other houses up the slope, between Marelle's house and the wall, and three more farther down. None of them were quite so fine as hers, but each had high walls surrounding their orchards, and they all were strongly built. They clustered near the southwestern gate of the city, sheltered by a steep drop-off to the west, and the guard fort on the southern route. It would be safe to sleep there—as safe as anywhere a man could sleep beneath the sky, outside the gates.

These were things he had to consider, as an outcast. The wound on his forehead hurt enough that he could not ignore it, but even without the pain, Cete doubted it would ever be far from his mind. It was like a missing limb. It was like a missing soul. But while he was no longer a fighting man, he was still alive, and it was good to be alive, to see a sunset, to drink water, cold and sweet, from a stone jar.

After the sun set, and the valley below was glazed over with the cold moonlight, Marelle returned, two men and a woman coming up behind her. "Are you well?" she asked, kneeling beside him.

"No worse," he said, struggling to regain his feet. He had lain down before the congregation during his beating; damned if he'd do that again.

Cete had not been in Reach Antach long, and it was hard to recognize faces in the moonlight, when he usually saw them in the sun. But there could be no mistaking the gold and silver threads in the mantle, or the white hair of Lemist Irimin, scholar-priest of the Irimin school, made ghostly by the moonlight.

"Priest Irimin," choked out Cete. "I did not—"

"It is not customary for weddings to be conducted after nightfall," said Lemist. "But this is a matter of custom, not law. When the situation demands a late wedding, it may be conducted, and it is valid."

Cete looked over to Marelle, who colored, but gave no other sign of embarrassment. "I knew that I could not remain within the walls forever," she said. "So I laid away what I could, built a refuge. It is yours if you will have it, Cete."

He had been a hero in the morning, a prisoner before judges at noon, then a dead man, and now . . . now he was offered something so precious he had not allowed himself to think on it. "This is not just to escape the—"

"No," said Marelle.

"I will cause you sorrow, Marelle," said Cete.

"Yes," she replied.

"And you'll be hurt again because of me."

"Yes," she replied again.

"But if you will have me, I will give you my whole heart."

"Yes," said Marelle. "I know. That's why the priest is

here, and the witnesses." The light was not good, but Cete could see the corner of her mouth quirked up in a smile, hear the warmth in her voice.

The witnesses came forward, draped Cete in a white mantle and anointed his forehead with olive oil mixed with myrrh and rockrose, just below the cut Mase had made. Cete had seen both of these men; one was a younger cousin of the Antach, the other a scholar who sat near Lemist during the services.

"Have you a wedding gift?" asked Lemist as Cete drew close, to see Marelle with her hair tied up with a bride's ribbons.

Without thinking and for a second time, Cete un-hooked the clasp of his merit chain and offered it to Marelle. This time, she took it from his hand and, fumbling only slightly, put it around her hips, looping the excess twice before the clasp would close.

It was as short a ceremony as was allowed by law; Cete was too weak for anything longer. They swore the three oaths, and said the three prayers, had their wrists bound together by the priest, and had the strand cut by the witnesses. Then Lemist said a prayer for them, and the witnesses affirmed that all had been done according to the law, and then the priest and the witnesses left, headed back into the safety of the walls.

Cete looked over to Marelle. The mantle was damp

with blood against his shoulders, and the night had grown cold. She was looking slightly to the side of where he was standing, a small and strange smile across her lips. Cete was off his balance, and not because of his wounds. It was impossible that he was married, impossible that he was alive, and married to Marelle, with the wedding oil mingling with the blood on his forehead, the strands of the marriage cord tucked into the belt of his mantle.

"Are there any further reasons why you'll not come into your house?" she asked.

"My house," said Cete, slowly.

"Unless there is a divorce, or you die," said Marelle, "it's as much yours as it is mine."

Cete picked up the blankets she had brought out, and the stone water jug, and found himself light-headed. He reached out, took hold of her by her shoulder, and allowed the blind woman to lead him home.

It was warmer inside, and darker. Cete followed Marelle to the bed, the one he had slept on after she had rescued him. Light-headed again, and worse. He dropped the blankets, convulsed, vomited on the floor. Marelle knelt beside him, her arm strong enough to support the weight of his chest as Cete's strength left him.

"Too much of the wedding wine, too many of the wedding meats," she said. "You shouldn't indulge so freely, husband mine."

Cete shivered, gave another gasping retch. "I'm sorry," he said. "Probably not how you saw your wedding night."

"No," said Marelle. "But then, there are times that life gives you more than you expect." She helped Cete back into the bed, changed the dressings on his back. He fell asleep to the sound of her scraping clean the beaten earth of the floor.

Chapter 5

Cete did not sleep well that night. When he moved, either the scars burned, or he felt the unfamiliar weight and warmth of sharing a bed with a woman, a thing he had not done since his exile from the Hainst. As a result, he remained in bed half asleep and half awake until well into the morning, when a visitor came to Marelle's house.

He had seen her before, sitting among the scholars, but he did not know her by name. She was small and slight, but walked with a professional assurance, her hair in widow's braids.

"Blessings to the married," she said, as she came in. "I hear that the wounds opened during the ceremony."

"Before, during, after," said Marelle, acidly.

"I see," she said, coming over to where Cete lay. "If I could have a look?"

Cete pulled his shirt back slowly, wincing as the dried blood pulled loose from his skin. First the priest, with witnesses of high standing, then the Reach's doctor. There was no law that said that those who had been scarred on their foreheads were to be shunned, but they usually were. It seemed that in his case, things had reversed—if he had not been scarred, a junior scholar might have blessed his marriage, and a butcher or carpenter might have tried to set his wounds.

"Mm," said the doctor. "It is better than it looks; a weaker man would have been flayed to the bone with those strokes, but there was enough muscle there to cushion him. The blood flow seems healthy; it is clotting well, and your pulse remains strong despite what you have lost. I will again sew closed the wounds that have opened. It will hurt."

The doctor said the healing prayers, another thing not usually done for outcasts, and set to work. It did hurt, but not badly enough to matter. Marelle sat beside them, holding Cete's hand in her own; from how hard she grasped, it seemed like she was the one being sewn together. As the doctor worked, Cete considered what it all meant, and what he should do next.

"When you are done," he said, "will I be well enough to attend the afternoon services?"

The doctor paused in her work, considered, and then her needle flew again. "It would be pushing things," she replied, which was true in more than a medical sense. Outcasts were permitted to conduct business within the walls during the sunlight hours, to live within the walls during times of siege and other calamity, and to attend services with the congregation, but there were few who wore his scar who availed themselves of those privileges. The last in particular was done by few who were cast out for any reason, permanent or temporary—they had been removed from the community of God, their voice had been silenced in the choir. Outcasts who chose to pray did so on their own, concealed in the closet, or during the midnight hours.

"Give yourself a day, or perhaps two, to heal," she said. "After that, I see no reason to distance yourself from the congregation."

Cete swallowed back a yelp as the doctor pulled the needle through his flesh another time, tied off a knot. More dabbing with the blood-soaked towel, another blessing, touching the wound with an apricot twig wrapped round with hyssop. Marelle did not move throughout the procedure. She showed no fear of the blood, nothing but a tightening of her hand when the needle bit particularly deep.

"If the wounds show signs of festering," said the doctor, turning away from Cete and talking to Marelle, "change his bed so that it aligns with the door, and have him wear red or blue clothing, but never black or green. Also, he must not eat too much raw food, and should have greens and pomegranate with his meal, if there are any to be had. There will be some bleeding, but not too much—the wounds have already started to knit. To speed the healing, he should sleep as much as he can."

"Of course," she said. "Thank you."

The doctor gave a brief, awkward bob of her head, and left.

"Radan might let us be, if you don't push," said Marelle.

"If you want, I will not go to the church," said Cete. As soon as the doctor had started her work, Cete had started to think about pressing his feud against Radan Termith, and had not stopped to think about what Marelle would want.

Marelle was silent for a long time, her body still, next to his. "I suppose it is the role of a wife to urge caution, to try to convince you to give up fighting, to remain at home and to live to die in bed. Is that what you expect of me?"

Cete was silent just as long. That was what was expected of the wife of a fighting man, just as Marelle had said. The men in the ranks were supposed to leave behind women who wept at them to stay, who needed lies and cajoling before letting their men march out to war, and who cared less for war and honor than for home and hearth.

"Marelle," he said, finally. "I do not wish you to be anything other than what you are."

"Good," she replied. She let go of his hand, stroked

his cheek. "I cannot be. And neither can you. If you have the strength, go to the afternoon services. If you do not, wait, but no longer than you must. The Antach knows what Radan is, but he cannot say it. If you are seen, the blood on your mantle will say what it is forbidden for mouths to speak."

"He will kill us," said Cete. "When he sees that I am not shunned, and do not fear to show my face in the church. He will send men to kill us, to paint our house with our blood."

"Perhaps he shall," said Marelle. "But if we are going to die in the defense of Reach Antach, we should die as best we can. This will do more good than being burned in our house by tribes brought by the city clans."

Cete found himself smiling. That was what had drawn him to Marelle, that was what bound him to her. She fought. She fought to keep her art, she fought to keep her place in society, and though night rose up around her, she fought like a ten-year veteran with a waist covered in merit chains.

They could leave. Reach Antach was doomed, and nobody would blame them if they left. Even if they had no other savings, they would get a better than fair price for her house and orchard, and they could live somewhere else. Cete didn't bother to mention it. Anywhere else, they would be nothing more than outcasts; in the clan cities, wealthy outcasts could buy safety, the semblance of honor, but Marelle would be able to hear what people thought with every word, and Cete would see it in every eye. All that, for what? As Marelle had said, to live to die in bed?

"Board shut the windows," said Cete. "But leave a lamp lit, so that I can see how things are when I return. Draw three days of water from the well, and keep it in covered pots. If there is time, buy seasoned wood, and shape it into spear shafts."

Cete lowered his feet down to the floor, raised himself up. Marelle did not try to aid him; she let him stand on his own. He was weak, certainly, but not so weak as he had been the day before. "I shall go to the afternoon service," he said, "and I shall do my duty by you when I return, wife."

Marelle colored, a red flush rising in her cheeks, and in the pale places of her neck. "As you will, husband," she replied. As the proverb said, fruit tastes its best just before the rot. Life was best when standing in the shadow of death.

It was not a short walk from Marelle's house—from Cete's house, now—to the church, and he was weaker than he had supposed. Twice he had to stop to catch his breath, and towards the end, he could feel his back begin to bleed again. But he walked into the church when the scholars and priests were just finishing their additional prayers, before the general afternoon services.

Cete had sat among the guests during his first visit to the church of Reach Antach, and then among the captains of the Reach army. Now he sat in the section below the balcony, which was reserved for outcasts and criminals. As expected, none sat there with him, and as the church filled, his old seat among the army captains was left conspicuously empty.

Radan was sitting up on the dais, wearing a fine prayer mantle, all red and gold. He gave Cete a flat, expressionless look, and then turned his face forward and up, to God. The doctor saw him as well, gave a short shrug that managed to convey both disapproval and admiration, and turned back to her prayers. Then the congregation began singing, "the great God of beginnings and endings," and Cete joined them, joined the voices that rose up in the hymn of praise.

He had considered his own inclinations, and Marelle's, but now in the church, in the face of God, Cete was forced to wonder if he had right on his side. Radan had given orders—wicked orders, but that was on his soul—and Cete had disobeyed. Marelle had saved him from the full consequences of that, but the scar he wore on his forehead was rightfully given. According to law, he was an outcast. What then was he doing in the house of

God?

"The God who has taught us to love good and hate evil," they sang, women's voices mingling with men's, law mingling with praise. There was a requirement to love good and to hate evil. Tradition said that one should love before hating, and there was little love in what Cete was doing. Still, the law came before tradition, and what Radan had done—to take a contract with the intent of harming the one who purchased his labor, to conspire in the destruction of a reach, and the murder of the people of the reach—was evil. Cete was no scholar, but what he was doing was within the law.

The hymns ended, and the congregation stood for their silent prayers; some asked for health, or good fortune in their labors, with their families. Cete prayed for strength, and for courage, and for God to grant his blessing to what Cete intended to do. Then the Antach blessed the congregation, as did the priest, who spoke for a time on the laws of fasting season. Then came the closing hymns. The prayer had left Cete tired, so he sat for a time on the bench, gathering his strength for the walk back home. One of the captains general in the Antach clan army came up to him as he was sitting, his prayer mantle folded under his arm.

"Blessings to the married," he said. Cete had seen him approaching, but to hear him talk was so unexpected that

Cete started, did not know what to say.

"Thank you," he said, collecting himself.

"How is your back?" asked the captain general. "Are things well with you and Marelle?"

"The back is improving," said Cete. "And Marelle is well. Thank you." He was no longer under orders, but his replies were stiff, his back straight. It would be difficult to let go of the habits formed in a life under arms.

The captain bowed his head. "If you would not mind, I would walk you to the gates of the Reach. The day is hot, and you have lost much blood."

Cete looked up at the dais. The Antach was no longer wearing his prayer mantle. He did not seem so sleekly confident as he had been when Cete had sat among the guests, but he was freshly shaven, and he talked with the priest easily, showing no sign of nervousness. The priest seemed troubled, her eyes dark, and Radan was a thundercloud. So. Cete's gift had been understood, and accepted; the Antach would rub the shame of what had been done to Cete into the face of his general, until something broke.

"Thank you," said Cete. "It would be a comfort."

As they walked through Reach Antach, Cete and the captain of the Antach talked about the laws the scholar-priest had expounded, about the coming olive harvest, and some remedies the captain's family had passed down for keeping wounds clean, so they did not suppurate. Inconsequential matters, for the most part. The point was for them to be seen talking together.

Some of the men of the Reach came up and blessed Cete on his wedding, or asked this or that of the captain of the Antach. Others shut their doors as Cete passed, spat on the corner stones of buildings, or turned their eyes away. Perhaps they were partisans of Radan Termith, and opposed to the Antach. Or perhaps they did not wish to see a man scarred for disobeying orders walking the streets of their Reach.

When they reached the southern gate, the captain hesitated. "It's a dangerous time," he said. "And your lady wife is known as a fine hostess. If it is not too much of an imposition, perhaps some of my friends will stop by later in the evening, for the meal after the service."

Cete hesitated. It was a fine offer, and showed a generosity of spirit on the part of the Antach. All the same, if he were to accept a bodyguard of the clan army, it would undo much of what he intended. That he was not shunned in the church, that a man of standing chose to talk with him in the street, these were things that no court would hold against the Antach, no matter how corrupt the court might be. But if the Antach were to assign a bodyguard, that would indicate a lack of respect for the law, and a lack of respect for Radan, and give the Termith cause to march on the Reach.

"It is a kind thought," said Cete, "but I am afraid that we have not laid in provisions for guests; the marriage was a sudden one, after all. Perhaps in a week or two, when matters are properly arranged."

The captain did not mistake his meaning. He looked to one side, and then the other; there was nobody close enough to hear. "I thank you," he said, "and the Antach thanks you. But he bade me ask: Why?"

"Because of an embroidered mantle, and a blind woman's smile," said Cete, without thinking. He paused, considered the question properly. "Because I am a fighting man," he said. "I fight."

The captain shook his head. "You do," he said. "Like few men I've ever seen."

Cete shrugged. "Most aren't given a fight of this sort," he said. "Anyone in your ranks might do the same."

"I hope you are right," said the captain. "But what might be done is different from what has been done. Come what may, so long as any who love the Reach Antach remain living, you will be well regarded."

Cete bowed. There was nothing to be said to that.

"But I keep you too long from your lady wife," said the captain. "Go in good health."

"To you and yours," replied Cete, and he went down to the house that Marelle had built against the day she would be cast out. Waiting for him there was a meal of venison cooked with figs, of greens and pomegranate.

When the dinner was done, Cete did his duty by Marelle, as he had promised. He was long out of practice, and his back still ached and bled, but she was eager and kind, and his love for her was so great that all else was forgotten. Cete could not recall a time of greater joy, not in his youth, nor in his years of manhood. They were in that bed together for a long time, taking the sweetness of life in the shadow of death.

Chapter 6

The next day, and the day after, Cete did not go far from the house. Because they were lower on the slope than the houses next to the wall, the neighbors could see down into the fenced orchard. Twice they raised a cry of burglars, though everyone knew that the men who had climbed the fence were not there to filch unripe fruit, or to take wood contrary to the law. They would not be able to come during the daytime.

Cete slept in the day, and remained awake at night, a spear close at hand. For Radan to do what his clan had sent him to the Antach to do, he needed the confidence of at least some of the men of the Reach. Those who could not abide by what he had done to Cete were already lost to him; those who could swallow the abuse of the law would not be so ready to let pass signs of weakness. Going to church had been a challenge to which there could be only one answer.

Despite the care that Marelle took, despite the blue of his mantle and the pomegranate and greens with his meal, Cete's back still pained him whenever he took a sudden motion, or when he awoke from sleep. If he could, he would have left what needed to be done for a week, or even two. But if it was left too long, he would have to fight on his enemies' terms, where they chose. On the fourth night after his wedding, Cete stretched, tucked his axe into his belt, and went to the door.

"I fear the stones of some of the tree-gutters have come loose during the day," he said. "I'll go and attend to them."

Marelle was sitting in her high-backed chair, working some piece of embroidery. "Of course," she said. "Before you go, see your commission; I've almost finished it."

The house was in near darkness. It suited Cete well, and while Marelle could still see well enough to tell light from dark, she did not prefer the light. At that, though, Cete kindled a lamp, and brought it over to where Marelle was working.

She was sewing white thread on a white fabric. Silk thread and linen fabric, by the look of the cloth, and the way the thread shimmered in the lamplight. Marelle tied off the string, unfolded the cloth that she had been embroidering.

It was a funeral shroud. Cete took it from her, ran his hands over the design. Cypress around the border, with rabbits and owls in among the branches. Above the trees were all the stars of the heavens, perfect in their places.

It was as fine a work as the mantle. He could not have hoped for anything better.

He would wear it once, and only those closest to him as he was laid down in the earth would see the embroidery; from even a few feet away, it would seem a simple white cloth. "This does me too much credit," he said. He did not have so little regard for the honor of other men, his love of beautiful things not so untainted by a desire to be seen possessing them.

"No," said Marelle. "Not enough. But if the stones of the tree-gutters have come loose, you ought to see to them. I would not wish to lose the water when the rainy season comes."

"I will not be long," said Cete. "It is a small repair."

As he went out he took one of the spears he had prepared in the days since his wedding. Seasoned wood, and with a steel head he had spent long hours sharpening. It would serve.

It was a warm night, and the moon near full; it was almost as light outside as it had been within. Cete stood for a moment, enjoying the scent of artemesia and honeysuckle, and watching the shadows.

There were three of them, slinking like jackals in the shadows of the walls and trees. They had come into his orchard; they had made themselves free within his walls. He could feel his blood rising, the shaking of the hands, the tightening of the vision.

Three was too many, if they were any good at all. If he charged in, axe swinging, he'd be cut down. He let his shoulders slope, leaned against the spear as though he needed it to support his weight. It was not much of a performance, but it was what they'd hoped to see; perhaps it would be enough.

They came in, closer, their boots crunching down the summer-dry earth beneath the trees, the faint clink of mail audible over the distant hooting of an owl and the buzzes of the night insects.

Cete had not let himself feel rage at Radan Termith, and what the Reach general had done. It was too large a thing; there were too many ways his wrath would serve his enemy. But now, in Marelle's orchard, fury was rising up from where his toes gripped the earth, up the back of his spine. Three to slay one injured man, one blind woman? Three in armor? His anger filled him so full there was nothing else beside anger. The spear rose up in his hand, and he threw, no craft, no plan, his hand moving without any act of thought or will. He threw so hard that the spear seemed to flicker out from his hand into one of those shadows, catching the man in the shoulder and driving him back into an olive tree.

His axe was in his hand, though he could not recall pulling it from his belt, and he was in among the other two, though he could not remember crossing that ground. There was the ring of steel against steel, sparks from axe and blade. They did not expect anything like this. Cete had not expected anything like this. It was not the measured practice of morning or evening routine; it was not even the clash of arms on a battlefield. It was the clawing of a wild beast, injured in its lair.

He came in, and the sword of one of the men cut in along his arm. The pain was . . . it was become pleasure; he howled in the joy of it, struck out with his axe, cutting through armor and chest, laughed to see dark blood in the moonlight.

The other man stepped back when he should have stepped in, tried to line up a proper attack. Cete came in too fast for that, his axe swinging around, hungry. The man was pale in the moonlight; he held up his hand to stop the blow, rather than his axe or a knife. Cete's blade sheared through his fingers and buried itself in his shoulder. The man staggered back, screaming. Another blow with the axe, and he was dead as well.

Cete howled, a long, ululating cry more like a tribal yell than anything taught in the cities. It was not enough; three men were not enough. He had his axe in his hand and the pain in his arm, and there was a man in the city who was his enemy. He could go and slay, and glory in the slaying forever.

He breathed, once, twice, fought back the nausea he had felt at Marelle's bedside, that he had felt when Mase had been beating him to death. There was a constellation of pain from his back, there was a cut along the length of his arm, and there were two dead men lying at Cete's feet. This had been the madding, the real thing.

The hills still echoed with Cete's howl. The echoes sounded no different than what had burst from Eber Hainst, when he could no longer bear the leadership of the Hainst of the Hainst. It was well that he had not allowed the captain of the Antach's guard to keep watch over his house. If there had been anyone else standing in the orchard with him, friend or foe, that man would only have lived if he had killed Cete.

Cete walked over to the man whom he had hit with the spear. He was still standing, impaled—the spear had gone through the mail shirt, and the shoulder, and through the mail again, the head buried deep into the tree. The man shivered as he stood there, like a man struck with fever, or one caught in a snowstorm. Perhaps it was the wound, or perhaps fear. It didn't matter.

"Please," he said, as Cete came close. "Please, I had no choice! I—"

Cete pushed his head up and back, and took the man's throat out with the hook-bladed tribal knife he had won in the river-cut field. The men who had come to kill him and his wife were dead, but the business would not end if he took half measures.

From one of the trees beyond the wall, an owl hooted, and out in the valley beyond, a jackal yowled its response. There'd be meat enough for them, and soon. Cete wrenched the spear out of the dead man's shoulder, and let the corpse fall to the ground. The tip was bent by the impact, blunted. When he was done with his work in the garden, he would have to grind that down, if he wanted to trust the spear again.

With that done, he came to the door, which had been closed behind him. "Marelle?" he said, wearily.

There was the sound of the bar being moved, and then the door opened. Marelle flung herself forward like a stone from a sling. If he had not caught her, she would have fallen, she was moving so fast, and she could not see.

Cete caught her and held her, his arms wrapping around her, heedless of his cut, of the pain caused by the way the skin stretched. She stood in his arms, and wept, beautiful in the moonlight.

They stood there for a time, beneath the stars, and said nothing. Finally, Marelle's shudders grew fewer, she gained control of her breath. "How many?" she asked.

"Three," said Cete.

"There will be more next time," she said. "He can't—"

"Perhaps," said Cete. "But while Radan cannot let this

lie, he also cannot look too much a fool. I will see what I can do."

"Within the law?" asked Marelle, drawing away slightly.

Cete hesitated. "At the edges," he said. "A scholar would be more certain as to which side it lies."

"I understand," said Marelle. "Do you need help?"

"No," said Cete. Marelle's face closed up, and he hurried to explain. "It's butcher's work, and I know the meat, and where to make the cuts."

"I will stand with you, and I will do a portion of the work," she said, and Cete turned away, ashamed to have misunderstood, to have rejected her help when she offered.

"Of course," he said, taking hold of her by the arm. Cete led Marelle to where the bodies lay, gave her the fingers he had severed, and told her to take them and leave them on the trash heap beside the back gate of the orchard fence.

When she returned, he guided her hand for one stroke with the axe, to start the work of severing a hand at the wrist. "Thank you for your help," he said. "I think I will be able to do the rest of the work myself."

She gave a nod. "Yes," she said. "And do see to the tree-gutters. There is too much work during the harvest to see to their repair, and the rains come on the heels of the harvest."

Cete watched her as she walked back to the house. The little work she had done had stained her hands with blood, down to the wrist. If he was in the wrong, she would stand beside him before the judges. It was a heavy responsibility that she had laid upon him, but in truth, it was upon her all along. They were husband and wife now, and the risks he took were now hers as well.

As he had said, it was butcher's work, and he knew the meat. It was not too long before the men who had come into the orchard were cut apart and lying on the dungheap beside the wall. The rest of Radan's men would hear, and learn what fate waited for assassins in his service. It would be answered, assuredly, but perhaps ... well, he would go to church for the morning service, and see if his decision had been wise. After he attended to the tree-gutters.

Chapter 7

The next day, there were men wearing the colors of the Antach clan army playing dice in the shade of the city gate. They did not bid a good morning to Cete, or extend to him blessings on his marriage, but they were close enough that if Radan attempted to have his revenge on Marelle, they would see it, and would have no reason to refrain from sounding the alarm. Good.

In the street, some of the men he had seen in the Reach army gave Cete looks that made him regret the law that outcasts could not walk armed in the streets of the Reach, except in times of siege. But there were others who stood up in respect as he passed. They did not say anything to him, but they walked beside him, in the direction of the church.

For most of the men of the Reach, Radan's attack on his former fifty-commander would seem a petty, vindictive feud of a man who had been in the wrong. What Cete had done was the sort of insult that men who counted themselves men would answer with a duel. But the Reach general couldn't duel an outcast; he'd lose just by starting the fight. Trying again with more men might work, but he'd look even worse. And if a second attack failed, his command would fall apart, and the Termith would have nobody to blame besides their scion.

It was the duty of every man to attend the morning service, but there were no penalties assigned for a week-day service. Most men attended most days of the week, but there was always work that needed to be done, men who awoke impure, men who had drunk too deeply the night before, and so on. On that morning, after Cete arrived, the church filled as though it was Sheavesday, or the Night of Sighs.

Even the benches for criminals and outcasts were full. Some of Marelle's neighbors were there, men and women whom he had seen in passing, and others who dwelt on the outskirts of the Reach Antach. Sitting before them were men who wore the bracelets that showed they had committed sins such that their labor had become the property of the Antach—mine workers and dung-cart drivers and tanners.

They did not look at him, for the most part, but when he prayed, they prayed with him, lifted their voices to follow his, fell silent when he was silent. Dangerous allies to have, a dangerous following to have gathered. Again, Cete considered the question of whether he had done wrong, whether his congregation of sinners reflected a well of sin within himself, from which they had come to drink. He did not think it did, and besides, there was nothing else he could do. His scar was no shallower than theirs; he had no right to consider himself above them.

The Antach attended to his prayers throughout. In the past, when he had finished a section before the congregation, or when an elderly and respected man had come up to the dais, the Antach would pause in his service, say a few words, reassure the congregation with nods and recognition. On that day, he prayed, and the prayer mantle he wore was a simple one, decorated only with the Antach seal in silver thread. It seemed that Cete was not the only one who had come to church to speak to God.

Radan Termith, on the other hand, wore both gold and silver in his mantle, and faced the congregation full on, his lips moving silently in the prayers. He had been angry with Cete before, but angry like a man gets angry with a rat for stealing his grain, or with a boar who had gored a favored hound. Now, Cete could feel the heat of Radan's rage, and he basked in it. All Cete had ever known was the life of a fighting man, and Radan had taken that away. It had been Mase's hand on the blade that had scarred him, but it had been Radan's arm behind it. Radan Termith had caused Marelle to be cast out as blind, he had sent men to kill them in the night. Cete's hatred for Radan had at last earned itself a mate in Radan's hatred for him, and those hatreds burned so true that it was the nearest thing to love.

So deep was his joy in the hatred of the Reach captain that Cete almost missed the beginning of the scholar-priest's reading of the law. As soon as the subject became clear, he immediately focused. "If a man should lead another man astray, so that the second man sins, the fault is in the second man," said the law. "Follow not where you are led, unless the law be with you." Well enough, but Lemist brought in another law—the law of a man who leads a congregation astray. Such a man is a public menace, akin to a wolf or hyena that has come within the walls of a city. He shall be put to death by the axe, and also his family shall bear the sin.

"But what," asked Lemist, "is a congregation? The Ayarith school teaches that it is ten men, and the ancient school of Baern says seven. But among the Irimin school there is a tradition that even three men, if they are drawn in together into the same act, by the same person, that is a congregation, and a man who has led three men into the same wicked act shall be put to death by the axe, and also his family shall bear the sin."

All the crowd in the church was silent. Perhaps there were some who did not know against whom this study of law was aimed, but they knew better than to ask questions, when they saw the frozen faces of those who heard what was being said. Cete looked back to Radan Termith, and for the first time, he saw that his enemy was afraid.

Lemist went on, explaining that according to the law, the "family" of a man who bore a clan name included the elders of the clan. Not that they were to be put to death by the headsman's axe, but bearing the sin meant living as outcasts for three years. And that while there might be disagreement among the schools as to the precise definition, all the schools would uphold the ruling of a properly appointed judge, even if the ruling went contrary to what their school taught.

Cete blinked, as the world spun around him. Lemist could not have risen so high in the Irimin if she was inclined to speak rashly. Tradition held that the schools would not involve themselves in clan feuds unless the law was too flagrantly violated, and it seemed that Radan had crossed that line. Lemist Irimin was old, and she was a woman; most schools did not allow women to wear the mantle of scholar-priests. It was easy to see how Radan would not have expected attack from this line. Cete watched the scholar-priest expounding the law, as though discussing a fine point of the construction of prayer altars, or of which crops are obligated in the tithes to the poor and which are not.

Each word was a hammer. By forcing Lemist to declare a man outcast, to participate in what was intended to be a judicial murder, Radan had made an enemy. Sending assassins after a man who could no longer rely on the protection of the Reach had caused a rage as deadly as any madding. For all that Lemist Irimin was old, and for all that she was a woman, she was a properly appointed judge; Radan had taken his case to her for judgment. There was no school that would fail to uphold her ruling, should she give it.

One slip, one more push, and Radan Termith could destroy the Termith clan with far greater ease than he could the Antach. If the men who had sent him out heard any of this, they would shit themselves in fear, and bury Radan so deep that he'd attend resurrection baked like an apple by the heat of the underworld.

This was not what Cete had intended. He thought that by pushing the edges of the law, he would once again be brought before the judges. The crime would have been a minor one, and after Radan had sat in judgment and agreed to a punishment, he would not have been able to pursue further vengeance without showing his contempt for the court. But it seemed that Radan's failure to account for the scholar-priest of the Reach Antach had already done the work required.

Cete rose mechanically for the closing prayers, as the sounds of the hymn were all but drowned out in the low hum of conversation. A weapon like this could change the whole situation. If the Irimin school were to come in on the side of the Antach—but no; they had not committed themselves. There was no talk of bringing Radan before the judges. For now, it was just a matter of law, read during the morning services. It was a warning, and it would keep Cete and Marelle alive for a day or two, at least.

Unless Cete could find some way to force Radan to lose control. Cete had felt it slipping during the morning service. There was a man there, wearing the mantle of the General of the Reach, and that man had been frustrated and embarrassed, he had lost when he had expected to win, and then lost again. If Cete could push him just a little further, find some other way to speak to his soul rather than to his mind, Radan would crack, and they would fight man to man, madding to madding.

Marelle was of the same mind when Cete returned and told her what had passed, but neither of them could find a way that would draw Radan in, when he would have set his mind towards keeping away. Cete pulled the boards from the window, shifted the bar from the door. If they did not need to fear the arrow by day or the knife at night, it was better to have some air than not.

After a time, three men wearing the white robes of judgment came, to remove the bodies from the dungheap. When he had set them there, Cete had thought to bar the court access to the remains. They had come by night, and sought his death; let their families come, and ask a ransom for the meat their men had left behind—if the butchery had not crossed the line of the law, that might have. But now, he let them in, gave them leave to search the orchard for pieces of the dead men that had been carried away by owls and crows. Now he was sheltering beneath the wings of the Irimin school, and he could commit no sacrilege.

"The Antach could have our murder done," said Marelle, when Cete returned. "What one man tells the soldiers of the Reach, another can just as well, and the court would not view Radan's pleas with any great favor."

"Mm," said Cete, and considered the possibility. "It would be a dangerous move," he said, finally. "What one man says, another hears. It would be difficult for him to do that, and wake in the morning without the weight of blackmailers resting upon his shoulders, and informers to the Termith buzzing in his ears."

"We could do it," said Marelle. "And free him from the weight."

It was a hell of a thing to suggest. To kill his wife of less than a week, and then himself, in the hopes that it would do more damage than they could alive. "If you wish this," he started, and then stopped. No, he would not turn the decision over to Marelle, act as though he had no voice. "No," he said.

She was silent.

"No, even if it would mean that we would triumph where otherwise there is only defeat, and not because our lives are too sweet to leave behind. Until this point, I have been true, and I will not end my life with a lie."

Marelle had stopped her embroidering when she made the suggestion, and now she started again. "I understand," she said. "I will not suggest it again."

Cete walked over, kissed her lightly on the forehead. "You are clearer about this fight than I am," he said. "And braver than any man I have known. But we have not yet lost."

"Of course," said Marelle. "What will you do next?"

"There is work to be done in the orchard," said Cete. "Some of the trees could use pruning."

"Of course," said Marelle, again. "I hope it does not prove as difficult as seeing to the tree-gutters."

Cete shrugged his shoulders; they still hurt, though they were not so ready to bleed. "I hope so as well," he said. All the same, he took a spear with him as he went out, and kept his axe close by in his belt.

From within the walls of the orchard, he could see the men from the Antach clan army up by the gate, and the neighbors on the slope above working their own fields.

It seemed unlikely that Radan would attempt anything, and if he did, there would be some warning. So, for a time, Cete put aside his spear, and worked in the orchard.

It was obvious that Marelle had hired men to work her orchard for her, and it was just as obvious that they had taken advantage of the fact that she could not see. The trees had been sloppily pruned, and there were dead branches left untrimmed. Olives were hardy, but dead wood attracted rot and worm, and it had to be taken out. It was hard, straining work, but it needed doing. Besides, for all that he had proven himself the better of three picked men, Cete would never again have a contract as a fighting man. He needed something else, and work among the trees was what he had.

Later in the day, Marelle came out with bread and fish sauce, and a pitcher of cool water, and it tasted as fine as a banquet, or as field rations after a battle was won. Then it was back to the trees, until there came the sound of a distant trumpet. Cete tied the bundle of dead wood he had gathered and waited until he heard it sound again.

Marelle was at the door. "The Reach army," she said. "They are heading out." Her ears were finer than his. Cete looked up. Late in the afternoon, but not too late to begin a march. The heat of the day was past, so they would make good time.

"I will go see this," he said, and he went.

As he passed through the town, the trumpets grew louder, and he could also hear the piercing trill of regimental horn. Marelle had been right. At the north gate, the crowd gave way before him, so he was able to see the army marching out, banners flying, with Radan Termith at their head.

The Antach stood atop the gate, his arms outstretched in blessing. He could do nothing else, for all that he knew what Radan was, and what would happen to any man in that army who remained loyal to the Reach Antach or Clan Antach. Cete watched, and counted. The ranks were thinner than they ought to have been. It seemed that some of the men in the ranks knew what Radan was, and chose not to bare their necks for his blade.

Not much thinner. There were those who were with the Termith against the Antach, and there were those who did not guess at what Radan intended. But there were also those who knew they were marching to the slaughter, but marched regardless, banners held high, eyes dry of tear, but filled with the awareness of death. Fifteen of the men whom Cete had trained and led were of that group; they carried the banner of the fifty that had been his, and they marched in good order. There was nothing to be said when faced with courage of that sort, of obedience to law and contract in the face of death.

Cete watched for a time, and then left. It hurt too much to stay.

When Marelle heard what Cete had seen, she was not surprised by any of it. "He was losing too much by staying in town. We forced him to move sooner than he would have liked." She was working on Cete's shroud again, putting the final stitches on the border. "There were weapons and arms to be found in the orchard last night. You should sell them."

Cete was taken aback. Three of them against an injured man, and they had come by night, and yet he had killed them all. That was a triumph worth celebrating. When there was time for it, he had thought to hang the armor from the rafters, use the axes in the orchard and the knives in the kitchen, and there would be nothing that the families of the slain could do but burn with the shame of it. And yet, he had eaten of Marelle's food, but had contributed nothing.

"We have a feud that is large enough for both of us," she said. "We do not need to pile smaller feuds on top, get distracted by fights which mean less."

Cete growled softly, shook his head. It went against every instinct, but she was right.

"I am not a fighting man," she said. "And I am not a clan lord. And it is not the money. If you like, you can throw what the sale earns into a well, or bury it beneath the floor. I have silver enough for our needs, and more."

"No," said Cete. "I think I have a purpose for silver, and this should meet my needs."

Marelle nodded and continued her work, and Cete went out to buy and sell.

As he expected, it was the easiest thing in the world to find buyers for the weapons and armor the men had been wearing when he had killed them. The families had no legal claim to the tools of their slain men, and they would not wish to bear the shame of them hanging as trophies in an outcast's house, beyond the walls of the city. He asked a merchant for double what they were worth, and the woman paid without hesitation—she would get triple when the families heard they were available for purchase.

Two hundred and seventy freshly minted marks, each of full weight, stamped with the seal of the Antach clan. Fair pay and more for a night's work, though it hurt to claim it.

On the south and east of the wall that Marelle had built around her orchard was a terrace wall, and below that, there were olive trees and apricot standing on narrow terraces. Too young to bear much fruit, they were an investment in the future of the Reach. To the west, though, was a fine orchard, fifteen trees all more than twenty years old, planted before the land was sold to those forced to live beyond the walls. A perfectly flattened piece of land, and the trees were widely spaced. Beside the olives it looked as though there had been a stand of timber trees that had recently been harvested.

The land and the trees were worth two hundred and fifty. Cete paid all he had gotten from the sale of the weapons, and was happy to see the money go. The saying was that silver forgets its fathers, but he remembered, and he did not want to feel the sale of trophies rightfully earned when he held those coins.

With the money paid, he and Marelle paced out the borders of his land with the old owner, and with his neighbors on all sides. It was a good purchase, though it might mean having to hire help when work needed to be done. But he had not bought the land for its trees, or for growing up a stand of timber to sell. When the neighbors had drunk the water and the wine to show that they were all in agreement as to the borders, and when everyone else had returned to their homes, Cete paced out a circle in the land that had been used for timber, and began to practice with his axe.

As a fifty-commander, he had practiced his routines daily, but he had not had a chance since. The healing skin of his back pulled and ached as he moved, but the cuts were sharp, and though his legs and arms complained at the twists and rises of the routine, they did not fail him.

He practiced from late in the afternoon into the evening, until after the sun had set. Then he returned to his house, where Marelle had laid a table on the roof, so they could take their meal in the cool of the night.

"The neighbors were impressed," she said. "It has been a long time since they have seen the fighting routines properly performed."

"Mm," said Cete. Fighting men were no more or less likely to be cast out from a town than others, but those that were seldom practiced. There was no law against it, but there were those who thought it defiled the routines. "If they wish to join me, they can. There is a good deal of space in our newly acquired land."

Marelle was silent for a time, as they ate their lamb with pomegranate. "I will let them know," she said. "Oh, Cete. You are taking a grave risk, yet again. I know what is expected of women, and again I tell you: I will not take the strength from your arm, and I will not counsel you to give up when there is fight left. I do not want a single hair on your arm to think of safety rather than war. But you can see why those weapons had to be sold."

Cete stiffened. Those men had come by night to kill. It was wrong that their families could sleep well at night, that they would be able to pass the harness to a younger son, to give the axe in a dowry, as though there was honor still left in the steel. "When a man fights," he said, slowly.

"The motion comes from the hips, the strength from the lower belly and spine. Perhaps I think too much with my lower belly and spine, but I can do no other. It is who I am."

"I know," said Marelle. "And I love you for it. But I am not a fighting man. And it is customary for fighting men to serve a lord, a position seldom reached by those who think with their spinal cord and lower belly. If you wish to feud, I cannot stop you. But I tell you not to feud, and I warn you that if you do, Radan's men will use it against you."

She was right, but he didn't like it. "I hope they do not use that bait on me, my wife. I will try not to bite, if they do."

"Thank you," she said, and extended her arm for him to take. There were rush mats up on the roof, for sleeping when the weather was fine, and now that the priest had made his threat to Radan, it seemed they could sleep there securely. Cete led his wife over to the mats, to do his duty by her. She pulled him down, held him; tender and demanding, soft and strong. It was a moment of glory, beneath all the stars of heaven.

Chapter 8

It did not take long for the word to spread that Cete was rehearsing the fighting forms in public, and had invited all who wanted to join him in the practice. They were the rightful property of all men, but for most the practice was dropped when it became too demanding, when youths became men, and the days filled up with other concerns. Now the news of what Radan meant to accomplish was spreading. Sickle heads were being beaten into daggers, axe heads were being polished and fitted with new hafts. And men who now felt the absence of martial training were looking for instruction.

The Reach army had left with no more than a week's rations. There was no hope of turning the masses of Reach Antach into a force that could oppose them in that time. But the fighting forms were a foundation. They taught the cuts and the blocks, pressed them into the mind and the muscle. Cete went through them, time after time. Morning form, evening form, the variants for holiday and public fast, again and again.

Some of those who came to participate fell out after

a few repetitions, returned to their homes or to their work. Others remained until they could not continue. Cete was no commander, no hired teacher, and he was careful never to act as though he were; when he offered a correction, it was always, "I have been taught this," and never, "You must do that." The people who attended learned, for what good it would do.

That is, the people who had come to learn learned. As Marelle had predicted, there were some of Radan's men left behind in the Reach, and as Marelle had predicted, they did not leave Cete to teach the fighting forms in his orchard in peace. Two different men tried to trip him, another let his axe slip at a critical point, so that it went skipping out where Cete had been standing. It was the hardest thing in the world to let that pass, to continue to teach in the face of insult. Cete had the tribal dagger in his belt, and it leapt up into his hand, as though it had a will of its own.

Each time, he forced it back to its sheath. The attacks were blatant enough, there were witnesses enough that if he called them on it, the law would probably be with him. But then he would spend two days, three, making his claim before the judges, one of whom would have been appointed by Radan to sit for him when the army was in the field. That Marelle was right didn't mean it was easy to do what she had told him.

Then came Mase, and Cete could feel the madding throbbing behind his eyes, had to fight to keep control of his hands.

The sergeant was careful, and cleverer than Cete had expected. He had brought along a jug of wine, and he sat himself down beyond the line of Cete's land, in the path between the fields. He didn't say anything, just laughed when one of the shopkeepers or outcasts or other students made a mistake. It wasn't long before he was joined by one of his cronies, and soon the two were pointing, calling out the beat incorrectly, and laughing when people fell, or missed their turns.

The men who had come to learn were working in a field where they had little familiarity. As stonemasons or fig-cutters they had expertise, but here they did not—otherwise, they would not have needed Cete's example. Men who are working beyond their familiarity, with no contract or lord's order—their morale was shaky, and there are few weapons so insidious as laughter, as the fear of looking a fool. The crowds which had been growing started to shrink, and those who remained grew even more uncertain in their steps, which led to more hilarity from the side.

"I think that I shall take a break," said Cete, "and study a section of the law."

"Whoo!" yelled Mase. "A scholar-priest! Everyone

quiet down, so we can hear the words of the scholar-priest!"

Cete smiled over at him. He had been winning, and he had his wine, but Mase flinched at that smile. Just a hair, but enough to tell Cete that Mase knew the line he was walking. "I cannot recall," said Cete. "But what is the law if a fighting man should leave his post upon the wall, and spend his time drinking wine beyond the city gates?"

There was laughter at that, and some of the joy left Mase's eyes. "Seventy lashes, and scarring, I think," said Jereth, a large and placid silver miner. Heavy work in the sun wasn't easy for someone carrying that much fat, but Jereth had kept at it, despite the heat and the mockery from Mase. "No," said Tarreer, a fig-cutter, who was some years too old to be a success as a fighting man. "If he leaves his post on the walls, that's death by fire. 'For the walls of a town are its men,' as the verse says."

"I'm not on duty, you thieves and prostitutes," said Mase, stepping forward. The man he had brought along was pulling at his sleeve.

"I think you're right," said Cete. "Drunkeness on duty is lashes, leaving a post on the walls is death by fire."

"There are people," said Mase, turning to his friend, "who are so ignorant of military form that they cannot tell the difference between a soldier on duty on the wall fifty, and a man on barrack duty." His friend laughed without any conviction that there was a joke there to laugh at.

"And what does one call a man who twice in a row finds himself on barrack duty, when the army marches out the northern gate?" asked Cete.

There was a silence from the men who had come to practice the fighting forms. This was no longer a joking matter, and none of them wanted to fight a duel with a sergeant of the Reach army, for all that he had found himself on barrack duty twice in a row.

Mase took another step forward. "This is a slander," he said. "And the law says—"

"So go thou and seek the judges!" roared Cete. He had been talking quietly throughout, while Mase had been blustering. Mase took a step back at that, looking pale. "See if they will hear your case."

Mase opened his mouth, shut it, opened again. He had been sent to harass Cete, but he seemed to have forgotten that there were three judges who would hear the case, and two were not kindly inclined towards Radan Termith. They would not listen to his plea, and Radan was not there to protect him from the consequences of annoying the Antach. He could attack, and when Cete killed him, then Cete would be forced to spend his time in court, rather than holding a court of his own. But it seemed Radan Termith had not bought that full a measure of loyalty from his man.

Cete laughed, loud and long, and Mase went from pale to flushed. "You look like a fish, Mase," said Cete. He puffed out his cheeks, opening and closing his mouth.

Mase took another step forward. His friend grabbed his arm and pulled him back, just beyond the line of Cete's property. As they started to argue in angry whispers, Cete turned, picked his axe up, and began the morning form once again, and the others joined in.

After a time, Abdelken, a mine engineer, half tripped on a difficult turn, and Mase began laughing yet again.

"Breathing at the right time is worth the concentration," said Cete. "For instance, you might want to try this turn more like a fish." He demonstrated, puffing his cheeks, opening and closing his mouth. The men who had come to learn laughed at that, and once again Mase went red. Twice more, he tried to disrupt the lesson with laughter, and twice more, Cete aped him, turned the laughter back at its source.

Then Mase left, and Cete loosened his knife in its sheath. It would not be what Radan had ordered, but Mase had left in a rage, and there was always the chance that he'd come back with more men, and that there would be a riot. Though Cete had been as cautious as he could, this probably came closer to feuding than Marelle would have wanted. Nothing to be done about it, and besides, if he had taken too many insults, he would not have had enough weight in people's minds for them to come to his field to practice their forms.

Not long after Mase left, a few more men came to stay and watch. They were not wearing their colors or armor, but they were men of the Antach clan army. Cete had seen them at services, and at practice. Preempting a riot by Radan's men, perhaps, or merely curious. Either way, they were there and watching, which meant that he could move to the next step.

When Marelle came out to bring him bread and wine, she asked if there was anything else she could bring. "Poles," said Cete, "of seasoned wood, each the length of a spear. A few dozen, if you can find them."

It was a difficult thing he had asked her to do, considering her blindness, but she made no objection, and it wasn't long before she came back with some of her neighbors, carrying the poles. Cete weighed each one in his hand, rejected a handful, cut off the ends of a handful of others, as the people who had come to practice rested in the shade against the heat of the day.

When he was done, he took up one of the poles and began a routine. There were spear routines, most commonly practiced in the eastern cities, but also among those cities and reaches who could not afford the metal for axe or sword. The form Cete was demonstrating was an eastern form, commonly used in the evening service, but stripped down to its most basic essentials. None of the broad movements of a single spearman, no casts, no rapid revolutions. It was almost a child's routine, but the pole was heavy, and the sun was hot, and all eyes were on him; difficult enough, for all its simplicity.

After the third repetition, one of the men picked up a pole and attempted to follow along, and soon after, more. Then he was going through the routine with the whole group doing their best to follow along. A few hours later, Mase showed up again, with five of his friends at his back. They saw the Antach's men standing about, and got into an argument with them. Cete was immersed in his work, and couldn't follow it completely, but what he saw from the corner of his eye showed that Mase and his friends kept their hands away from their weapons, and their voices low. Then they left, grumbling angrily.

It seemed that his work during Radan's absence was unlikely to earn Mase much gratitude, but that wasn't Cete's problem. He had to deal with men who were not accustomed to arms trying to learn a new form, with a new weapon, in the sun. All that without giving orders, or having any real authority. Every correction couched as a suggestion, every instruction phrased as advice.

It was nearly impossible work, but there was a need, and Cete worked until the sun was low in the sky. There was no hope of teaching those men enough that they could match fighting men, or tribal warriors. But they could learn to hold a spear, and they could learn to stand down a charge, keeping their spears braced. A spear thicket, even a thicket of shopkeepers and miners, could break a charge, and leave a force of fighting men a pile of corpses, if it would hold its ground in the face of death, if it could stand and not break.

When the day was done, Cete joined Marelle on the roof for the evening meal, and for the rush mats afterward. Later, they lay there together, her head nestled on his chest, and his hand idly moving through her hair, and he told her of the events of the day, and his hopes for the next.

"You will need more ground," she said. "We could cut the olives down, or buy the land to the east."

"No," said Cete. "There is a limit to how many I can teach, and I am near that number. Perhaps I can—"

Just then, there was a knocking on the door below. Marelle stiffened against Cete, as he disentangled himself.

"If they have come to kill you, I would not expect them to knock," she said. "Nonetheless."

"Mm," said Cete. He dressed, tucked his axe into his belt, loosened the knife in its sheath, and went down. Marelle's house had not been his home for long, but already he was so accustomed to it that he did not need light to know where to step. He came to the door, silent, and opened it just as another knock came, his hand just below the head of the axe, ready for a quick draw.

It was one of the Antach's men, wearing his armor, and his colors. "Blessings to the married," he said.

"Thank you," said Cete.

"If you are not otherwise engaged," said the man, "there are those who would have words with you, in your outer fields."

Cete hesitated. If he was led beyond the walls of his orchard and killed there, it might be passed off as something other than a conspiracy. And if this was what his enemies intended, a man in the Antach's armor would be the sort of tool they would use.

There was another man in armor waiting at the gate. It was hard to see in the moonlight—the moon was on the wane, so the light was not as good as it had been on his wedding night—but it looked to be the Antach's armor and crest as well.

"I do not—" started Cete.

"Please," said the Antach's man. "It's important."

The sensible thing to do was to stay behind, to bar the door and barricade the windows. And yet, there was the note of truth in the man's voice.

"Very well," said Cete. "I will follow."

There were two men standing guard by the gate and a dozen men in full harness out in the orchard, standing amidst lit torches. There, beneath the trees where Cete had spent the day teaching fighting routines, sat the Antach of the Antach, and Lemist Irimin, and the general of the Antach clan army, all wearing the mantles of their office. They were seated in high-backed chairs, and there was one there waiting for him.

There was the same sense of the earth whirling around him that Cete had felt when Radan Termith had called him to judgment for disobeying his orders. Calling him out beyond his walls made sense, at least—the house of an outcast was impure, and neither the Antach nor the scholar-priest could enter the walls of his garden without having to fast for two days, without bathing or anointing themselves. There was no time for that now, so the orchard was a fair compromise.

Cete took his chair, arranged his mantle around him as he sat. For a moment, he regretted not having worn the sunset mantle when he had left his house. Oh, but it would be glorious in the torchlight, for all that it would be an act of supreme folly to be anything but humble in the face of his visitors by night.

"Blessings to the married," said the Antach, and there was a low murmur of blessings from the others assembled.

"Thank you," said Cete. "Welcome to my fields; they and I are yours."

"Thank you." The Antach leaned back, looking at Cete. The torches left deep shadows, and Cete could not read his expression, but the way he sat in the chair, the tension in his arm, the angle of his shoulder, they all conveyed interest and authority. It was only because of the shadows of the torches that he looked sad, and afraid.

"I owe you a debt of gratitude," said the Antach. "The general of the Reach is allied with the enemies of the Reach, and you traded your honor to protect me from him."

Cete looked quickly around. The guards the Antach had brought with him were all standing beyond the borders of his land—far enough away that they would not hear the conversation, but close enough that they could respond to any attack. A clever piece of business; if there was a spy hiding amidst the shadows of the trees, he would hear what was said, but he would also be in another man's property after dark. The word of a trespasser could not be accepted in court.

"And you haven't stopped fighting on my behalf since," said the Antach. "We have few enough allies, and of those which we have, few have served me as well as you have, though you are no longer under orders, and though you owe me no debt."

"Thank you," said Cete, keeping himself back in his chair, cautious, not bowing at the compliments.

"You've not met my son," said the Antach. "Cete, this is Kern Antach, the general of the clan army."

Kern bowed in his chair, and Cete replied in kind; it was time for caution, not rudeness. This display, this honor being done, for all that it was done in secret—there was something the Antach wanted.

"It is on my advice that we are here," said Kern. He was very young, scarcely out of boyhood, but his voice was clear. "My taking the post of clan general was one of the conditions the Termith imposed, and while I cannot point to any great defeats, I fear they are not disappointed in my performance."

That was a hell of a thing for a man to admit—particularly a young man in a position of authority. Cete gave Kern a closer look. If he survived what was coming, this was a man who could make himself fit to rule.

"We would like to give you command of the forces of the Reach Antach," said the Antach.

The damnable shadows! Cete needed to see what that meant, but the light of the torches did not reach the Antach's eyes.

"Is this lawful?" he asked. "To give an outcast authority over men of a reach?"

"It is," said Lemist. "But it gives the opportunity for

violation of the law. Even in the heat of the battle, you must remember what you are, and what your position is."

That was why they had brought the scholar-priest; to confirm that what they were doing was within the law. If they triumphed on the battlefield, there would be the law courts to follow, and the Antach had his eye on that future, remote though it might appear.

It had been a mistake for Radan to use the priest in his play against the Antach. Cete could hear the faint echoes of anger in Lemist's tones. She had been forced to twist the law, to apply it on behalf of the guilty. It would be equally unwise for the Antach to make a similar mistake, and he was coming close to it. So long as they remained within the law, they might be safe.

Not safe. Cete immediately corrected himself. Even in the depths of his heart he could never count the Reach Antach safe. The Antach were a steer before the butcher, they were standing grain before the scythe. "Thank you," he said. "I will serve as best I can."

Kern passed a tightly wrapped parchment scroll over. "Your contract," said the Antach. "As Kern has said, his position as general of the Clan army is written into our contract with the Termith. He will retain command of my house troops. Similarly, Radan's contract is still valid. He still commands the Reach army and the militia."

"Mm," said Cete. "As clan general, are you bound to

listen to my orders, Lord Kern?"

"Not bound," said Kern. "That would be beyond the limits of the law. But any instruction you might give will be given full consideration."

Not the clan army, not the Reach army, not the militia. "I understand," said Cete.

When defeat looked inevitable, there were many who would take shelter in the church. There, by law and tradition, the conqueror would do them no harm. Depending on the provisions stored in the church, and the ability of their clan and kin to raise up ransom, they might leave in comfort, or into slavery, or into the ruin of a reach whose walls have been torn down, and whose houses have been taken stone from stone, to beg bread where they could find it.

Some would take refuge in the church at the first sign of a hostile army. Others might be induced to fight, and it seemed that Cete was seen as someone who might induce them. "The mustering ground is property of the militia," he said, "and its use would doubtless violate Radan Termith's contract. But I will need a field large enough that all the men who wish to fight can come, where I can see them performing the routines."

"It will be arranged," said the Antach. "Is that all?"

"No," said Cete. "The mine guards, and the caravan guards, and the troops of the private houses. By law and custom, you cannot command them, and private holders of fighting labor will need it now. But they can volunteer their services, if they are allowed by the holders of their labor. I need those men, and I hope you can get them."

"I will try everything I can," said the Antach. "Within the confines of the law."

"Thank you," said Cete. "I will also need spears. At least one for every man that will stand behind one, but better two or more, to replace those which break. Straighten the blades of bill-hooks, strip the iron from the doors of the Brotherhood Hall, but I need those spears. And I will need men to teach those who wish to learn. We have at most five days before a hostile army is camped at our gates. Your men have seen the simplified spear form that I was teaching; have them learn it, and have them use what time we have to teach it to whomever will learn."

"It shall be done," said the Antach. "You will want to see the contract by the light of the day before you take the position. But I do not think there will be anything in it to change your mind."

"Of course," said Cete.

"I am confident that I have made the right choice," said the Antach. "For once." He smiled, stood to leave. "There was one other thing that I had meant to ask you."

"Lord?" asked Cete.

"What sort of man was Eber Hainst?"

For a moment, all was quiet, even the crickets. "He was a great fighter," said Cete, slowly. "A strong man who could see clearly. He was constrained by his line's standing within the Hainst clan; he tried one thing, and then another, looking to join a new-founded reach, or lead a venture of his own, and was each time blocked by those who did not wish to see his father's line gain prominence. Thwarted ambitions fester. He lost none of his strength, but gave way to black moods, and in the end, to the madding."

"They gave you his axe and a merit chain, when he broke," said the Antach.

"And a banishment, to show that the lords of the Hainst had not commissioned the death of one of their own," said Cete. "I did what was needful, and paid the price."

"First for the Hainst, and then in my service," said the Antach. "You seem to pay a great deal, to do what is necessary."

"I've spent less than what twenty-eight of my fifty paid on the field," said Cete, "and less than fifteen of them are paying now, at the hands of Radan Termith. Less than many will pay, before the full moon next shines on Reach Antach."

The Antach bowed and left, with his son on one side,

and the scholar-priest of the Irimin on the other. A handful of the guards remained behind, their swords bared against the enemies of the Antach who might seek to kill his newest captain general.

Cete returned to the roof, where Marelle lay wakeful upon her mat, and told her what business had been conducted in the field he had bought.

"What do you think?" she asked, when he was done.

"I could not have hoped for more," said Cete. "But then, I could have said the same after my first meeting with Radan Termith."

"You think he will turn on you?" she asked.

"He may," said Cete. "It is one thing to give an outcast a command with no army. It is another thing to confirm that command when the crisis is past."

Marelle reached over and touched his face, looking to read something from his jaw, from his lips, from his neck. "You think that the crisis will pass?" she asked. "You think that we can win?"

It was not a question Cete wanted to face. "It is unlikely," he said. "The odds favor the Antach not having to make that decision," said Cete. He considered all the ways Radan could strike, all the resources the city clans would bring to bear, and the pitiful little the Antach could muster. "It's possible," he said, finally. "I don't know."

Marelle settled in beside him, her head on his chest. "Before Radan made his move, there was always the question lurking behind every sick sheep, every mine death, everything. Is this how the city clans will strike? Have they found a way to unleash a pestilence, will they poison the workers in the mines? It was a relief when you were called before the tribunal, in a way; I knew then how my death and the death of my reach had been arranged. If I allow myself to believe it, it will be strange to have hope."

"Mm," said Cete. "Very strange." Since Marelle had gone blind, she would have been living with the knowledge that she would be cast out. Since he had killed Eber Hainst, he had been a wanderer. If he allowed himself to believe it, to believe that what had happened in the garden brought with it the hope of a victory and the post of captain general of the Reach? Strange enough to break him like a twig, if it fell apart. When it fell apart.

Chapter 9

The stream that wound by the base of the hill on which the Reach Antach perched was mostly seasonal. It still had water, even in the depths of the summer, but little more than a muddy trickle. By the sides of the stream, barley fields stretched out in either direction, owned by the great families of the Reach. One owned by the Antach was given over to Cete as a mustering ground.

All the men who were between sixteen and forty years of age had passed before Radan Termith, and he had chosen one out of every ten to serve in the Reach militia. Some few paid instead of serving, filled their obligation with hired labor. The rest trained for two days a month in the mustering grounds of the Reach, and were given gifts at New Year's and at Sheavesday for their service; a portion of flour and of oil on Sheavesday, and a well-fatted lamb on New Year's. They drilled on the Reach mustering ground, and would be commanded by a lieutenant of Radan's if war came to the walls of the Reach.

Those who had been passed over by the Reach commander had mostly let their practice of the routines lapse, had let their ancestral weapons grow rusted, let the hafts of their weapons grow loose in their sockets. They knew this, and were ashamed, and very few wanted to show how incapable they were in public. And there was no portion of flour and oil for volunteers, no fatted lamb. Yet they came; three men out of every ten in the Reach, by Cete's estimation. By numbers, a larger force than that which Radan commanded.

Larger, but far less useful. With a handful of exceptions, they were not fighting men. Some knew the forms, some could even move with the axe or sword. But they shuddered at the noise of blade on blade, they feared pain and their heads were filled with everything besides what they ought to have been doing. Under most circumstances, there was nothing wrong with living like that. There were men who trained all their lives, and never fought; what advantage to anyone was all that training? But this was not a Reach like those, these were not men destined to live a life of that sort, and the lives they had chosen did not produce what Cete needed.

As with the fifty that Radan had given him, it was necessary to divide the troop. There were the caravan guards and family fighting men the Antach had managed to wrest loose from those who had bought their labor. A few who had been too sick to march out with the Reach army, but who had since recovered—perhaps two dozen men, all told. Added to that were those who had continued their practice, whose weapons moved where they willed them, some of the time. A handful of shepherds who knew the sling, a handful of miners who could stand and strike with sword and axe. One fifty of sling and javelin, three of sword and axe. The rest—and there were another nine full fifties of men who had shown up in that barley field below the Reach—would have to learn the spear as well as they could.

The men of the Antach clan army came down to the field as well, drilled the spear form with the men, practiced the sword and axe with those who could manage it, and tried to teach the slingers to throw in volleys. Cete prowled up and down the ranks as they worked, picked out men to serve as sergeants, as fifty-commanders. Tarreer had the skills and the attitude, but not the stamina. Jereth didn't have the necessary skills, but he would stand and fight, and his men would fight beside him; good enough. The best use of the Antach clan army would be as officers for the men he had been given, but that was not possible, so he did what he could, knowing that he was making more mistakes than proper decisions.

Better a mistake than a delay. The Antach had known that Cete would feel that way, and had slipped a few things into his contract that Cete would have argued, had there been time. Pay was too low for a captain general, for one thing, and the Antach had more authority over the men than a captain general's contract usually allowed, for another. It was reassuring, in a way—if the contract had been too generous, Cete would know for certain that he was not meant to survive the coming battle.

For the afternoon services, one of the scholars came down from the Reach, and led the prayers on the riverbank. Here, and here alone, Cete could stand at the front of a congregation, sit beside the priest as he gave his lecture on the law. It was not much of an army, but he was its general, and there was something to that, even if nobody who came down to wrestle recalcitrant spears in the summer sun would survive a single tribal charge.

After the services, the Antach came down with some of the servants of his house. The servants served out bread with olive relish, and pitchers of wine with water. Not a banquet, but a meal like that for nearly seven hundred men was no small expense. There were things the Antach of the Antach had done which struck Cete as foolhardy, but at least he didn't seem to be the sort to try to save bits of bronze while his house burned down. Except when it came to the salary for his captains general, but that was another issue.

"What do you think?" he asked Cete, gesturing with his chin towards the masses of men who had scattered to find shade at the edges of the field, to talk, and play dice, and to assert their freedom from discipline while they ate their meal.

"If they were fighting men," said Cete, "they would not be here. I can't hope to change that. All this—the drills, the formation, the assignment of sergeants and fifty-commanders—it is all to put enough blood in their livers that they will be able to stand in line, three deep, and remain with their feet planted against a charge. There are children of ten with enough strength to stand in the line, and to hold the spear in place, but it takes a man to see a charge of fighting men and bare steel, and to stand fast. They are not fighters, but there are men amongst them. We will see if they are enough."

The Antach nodded. "I had hoped they wouldn't be necessary," he said. "But my brother has been delayed."

Cete hesitated. He was a captain general, and it was traditional for captains general to argue with their lords on matters of policy, to speak freely when they saw mistakes being made. But he was not the captain of the Reach, nor was he a captain of the clan army. He was somewhere between a militia captain and a military advisor, neither of whom were traditionally given that sort of license.

"Your brother?" he asked, carefully neutral.

The Antach laughed. "Perhaps we ought to have

worked harder at concealment. But once it was known, it was known, and letting the news travel did him a great deal of good in the council-house of the White Horn tribe."

"His tribe," said Cete. "Even if he were not delayed, it will not be a single tribe that the city clans will have raised up against us." His hands were open, pleading; Cete needed his lord to give him more hope than this.

"The White Horns can put nine hundred armed men in the field," said the Antach.

That was something more.

"But as I said, they've been delayed. We shall have to hold until they arrive."

"If you'll forgive me for asking, lord—" He hesitated again, but if the Antach wanted to call him a captain general, he'd play the part. "Were you not expecting this?"

The Antach gave him a sideways look, with just a hint of a smile. They were away from the other men, walking in the field, where the furrows of the plows had been trampled down by the feet of the men who had been training. "The delay?" he asked.

"Among other things," said Cete.

"My brother anticipated an attack. They used sheep thieves, and most of those are hanging from their heels, out in the grazing lands. Some got away clean, damn them. But there were a few who were just a hair more clever; it took more time than expected to get the tribes to stop chasing those who looked as though they might be caught. It was a near thing, and did not work a quarter so well as the city clans must have expected. If we hold three days, my brother will be here." The Antach looked up to the northern hills, as though hoping to see a banner floating high and distant.

"As to the rest . . . it is easy to look at a prospect and see the benefits rather than the risks. And those who do not risk do not gain." The Antach gave a short shrug. "Every bargain we made was chewed over carefully before it was swallowed. Each one seemed like the best choice at the time, and yet it seemed that we swallowed enough unwholesome things to bring us down to the very edge of death."

Another sideways look from the Antach. "I realize that there is a great deal that I am not telling you, contrary to the usual custom of a clan chief and a captain general. There is little time for it, and nothing that can be done to change the decisions that have been made. But I will tell you this: The deal that the Termith offered seemed a far better one than Radan Termith gave to men he recruited as fifty-captains. And it has not quite served us so poorly as Radan's offers have served others."

Cete laughed. It ought to have stung, ought to have turned him inward from shame, but by saying that, the

Antach had opened up things within his mind that he had not been aware of. "Radan Termith has paid my bride price for the finest woman I have ever met, and made me the captain general of a reach. I do not forgive him what he has taken from me, but it would be difficult for anyone to look at what has gone to the buyer, and what has gone to the seller, and say that I made the worse deal."

It was true, and it was nothing but true, and Cete felt the edge of the madding receding. He was marked as an outcast, and could no longer find work as a fighting man. What he was had been taken from him. But he had become something else, something better.

The Antach stopped, and turned to look at him full on. "You will not be surprised to hear that I was urged not to hire you on as a captain general; to give you some other title, perhaps, or to let the opportunity that you presented pass by, because of the dangers in taking you on. Events will show who was right, and who was wrong, but I am glad to have met you, Cete; you see things clearly, even when honor and tradition ought to rise up to obscure your view."

Cete bowed his thanks, and the Antach bowed in reply, and left, headed back up to the Reach to make his preparations for the coming storm. Cete turned back to his men, tried to make them into the semblance of what they were not. He was forging a very specific tool, and if Radan did not do what Cete expected, it would be difficult to use his army for any other purpose.

At night, after they had eaten, but before they had retired to the mats, Cete told Marelle what he had accomplished that day, how the men had done, and how he had divided them. Some of his choices for command she endorsed, others she did not. Some of his mistakes could be corrected—they were not fighting men, and some would be happy to have the weight of command lifted from around their necks, if they were properly asked. Others would be enraged if the gift he had given was taken back. Those mistakes would remain until solved in battle.

When they finished talking, he took up Marelle's arm, and led her towards the mats. "Cete," she said, as they approached. "I wish for you to teach me the use of a spear."

He hesitated. There was precedent for women coming out to fight in defense of their homes, even in an organized fashion; in the battle of Long Winter, the siege had taken so many of the fighting men that there were fifty-commands of widows, all bearing the arms of their fallen husbands. "It is a noble thought," he said. "But you cannot fight; it would be too easy for a foeman to come up under your guard, to distract with a tap against the spear in one direction, and then to follow through the gap caused by a counter."

"I can die," said Marelle. "I would rather die in defense than in flight."

"No," said Cete. "When the trumpets sound, go to the church and stay there. Radan will not wish to stain the name Termith by slaying those who take shelter in the arms of God; it would undo all that the Termith sought to gain with his service."

"If I wait until the battle is lost, I will be trampled by those who move faster than I can," said Marelle. "If I go to the church too early, I will be thought a coward who has no faith in her husband."

"No!" said Cete. "The people who see you in the church will not be entirely foolish; they will know that you are blind, and that your early approach is because of that."

"And yet, it will be what they say about me, if you win."

He wanted to argue that point, but couldn't. "It is an unlikely possibility," he said. "Go to the church, survive the fall of the Reach."

"And then?" asked Marelle. "Live as a beggar in some strange reach, on the doorstep of some hold?"

"There is the silver you have earned with the work of your hands," said Cete. "But even if you cannot escape with anything more than your life, take it and go; yes as a beggar in some strange reach, or on the doorstep of some hold. Foul things have been done here by the city clans, and while you cannot fight with spear or axe, you can still fight them after the Reach falls. Rumor among outcasts will be heard in the halls of the mighty, and you can clothe Radan Termith in a mantle as perfect as the one you embroidered for him."

Marelle was silent, so Cete led her to the mats, and lay down beside her. "It would be too hard a life," she said, finally. "And too empty. I would rather die on the wall, with a spear in my hands."

"Not on the wall," he corrected. "The Reach army will have authority on the wall, and we cannot usurp that, without going beyond the bounds of the law. Before the wall."

He was silent for a long time after that, staring up at the stars. "It is better to live than to die, Marelle," he said, finally. "That is the word of the law. For me, I will live so long as I can, however beaten, however maimed. I will do good to those who love me, and harm to those I hate, so long as my lungs draw breath."

"If you think that I have not faced the choice of an easy death or a difficult life," said Marelle, "you are a great fool. I can no longer see the sun rise and set; I have never seen your face. But I am not a fighting man, and I am not so perfect in my obedience to the law. I will not hear Radan speak to me over your corpse, Cete. If you will not let me die upon the field, I will die in my house, amidst the flames."

"I would have you live," said Cete. "I do not wish to die, and know that I have caused your death."

"Then do not lose," said Marelle.

"It is in the hands of God, Marelle," said Cete. "Believe me; there is no way that I can fight harder. I will give this my all, and I doubt it will be enough. If you are in the field, I will have to decide between my duties as a captain, and my duty as a husband."

Marelle did not reply. After a time, Cete groaned, and pulled her to her feet.

"What is this?" she asked.

"In the first position," replied Cete, "your back leg is in a line with your spine, and it is pointed out." He adjusted her stance with his foot.

"Are you certain?" she asked.

"I have spent enough years practicing my trade to know the first position," he said.

Marelle snorted.

"If I thought that I could change your mind, I would try," he said, answering her actual question. "But I cannot. You asked me to teach you, and I will teach."

For the first time, she seemed uncertain. "You are right," she said. "I cannot fight. If I will harm the defense of the city, I ought not—"

"I cannot lie to you," said Cete. "I was lying by omission. You cannot fight well. But people will see you, and they will stand next to you. What I need from the men who volunteer to fight is that they stand to face a change, when every instinct tells them to flee. Perhaps . . . perhaps there are some who will not run, when they see a blind woman standing, weapon towards the foe. Not many; the fear that strikes in battle is too great to be understood. But perhaps some."

Marelle adjusted her foot to match Cete's correction. "Thank you," she said.

He groaned, and shook his head. "Marelle," he said. "I do not want to use you in this fashion. Do not thank me."

"Of course."

"And tell the other women to ask their husbands to teach them the use of the spear. Let the word spread that if women will come to fight, there will be a place for them before the wall."

They worked together into the night, Cete teaching Marelle as best he could, and Marelle learning as best as she was able.

Chapter 10

Cete had expected the army to reach their walls in three days. It took four days before the lookouts sounded their horns, and Radan Termith came up to the gates of the Reach Antach, his banners torn and bloody.

Despite his defeat at the hands of a coalition of tribes, and despite all that Cete knew, Radan Termith looked like a prince in defeat, like a true leader of men. From his seat in the back of the church, amidst the outcasts, Cete could not help but compare the two captains general of the Reach Antach, and know himself to look the worse. He was old, he was scarred, and there was the mark on his forehead, scabbed over but unmistakable. Radan stood tall at the dais at the front of the church, his eyes turned heavenward, his voice clear, his skin unmarred. To compare the two would be to compare allegorical representations of sin and virtue.

Cete knew that he slacked in his observances to God, knew that he was scarcely a model of virtue. But compared to Radan, an ape would look like an angel. It was astonishing that Radan would show his face in the house of God, after the work that he had done in the field. More than half of his command was dead or taken captive. Those were the men who were loyal to the Reach, the men who had marched out knowing that it was to their deaths or to the ruin of their lives. The first sin was the slaying of a man. Radan had reaped a harvest hundreds of times larger; he could scarcely doubt that the eye that saw that first killing, and which had judged then between the innocent and guilty, would have seen what he had done, and would judge him as well.

The tribes were hot on Radan's trail, of course. There were fires on the hilltops, there was the sound of tribal horn and drum even during the day. The Reach army had marched in before the afternoon service, and they marched out again the next day, just after the morning service, and arranged their lines all along the river below.

As the lines formed up, Cete watched from the tower of the Antach's palace, for he had no place to stand on the Reach's wall. If he had not known Radan Termith, he would have thought things well arranged. It was true that taking the low ground meant giving up the advantage of the Reach's walls, but it would make it difficult for the tribes to encircle the Reach without meeting the men of the Reach in battle.

Those looked like sound tactics. It was not yet Sheavesday. In most of the fields, the barley still stood, the fruit still hung on the branches of the olive trees. If the tribes were to complete the circle, and were to set a proper siege, it would strain the granaries. It would mean starvation for the poor, and want for the wealthy. Force the tribesmen to stand and fight, trade men of the Reach army for warriors of the tribes. That would prevent the circle from closing, that would put a strain in the coalition of tribes, give the reserves a chance to break the siege before it began.

Cete knew Radan Termith, and he knew that things were well arranged, knew that the tactics were sound. The Reach army was drawn up in ranks, with the militia behind them. When the army broke, they would stampede through the militia. Those who did not break would die, their lines in disorder. The rest would run up, climbing terrace after terrace towards the Reach, whose walls were undermanned, and whose gates would not be permitted to close.

Radan had marched out after the morning service, and arranged his lines in the field. If he had his way, the palace of the Antach would be cast down before the afternoon service, and the Reach Antach would provide a torch to illuminate the coming night. Whether these things would come to pass would depend on how many tribes the city clans had paid for, whether the Antach's brother would come in time, on all the chance and strength that came into every battle. Whether or not the Reach Antach would burn that night was in the hands of God. But whether it was the price of victory or the cost of defeat, Cete would make Radan pay his full measure before the day was out.

Cete came down from the palace of the Antach with his scar open on his forehead, and with his badge of office on his chest. He put on the sunset mantle that his wife had embroidered at the commission of his enemy, and went out to arrange the lines of his troops.

They came late, and they came frightened, and many of the men who had come to train did not come to fight, hiding themselves in their houses, or taking refuge in the church. There they would shudder at the sound of every horn, afraid also of the silences, when the horns' voices ceased. But men came, and men who had not come down to the orchard or barley field came with them, to stand with their spears in hand, beyond the gates of their city.

Their wives came as well. Not so many as the men, but some women took up spears from the armories of the Antach, wearing jackets reinforced with leather, their sandals laced up to their knees. If he failed, they would die, or be taken as slaves by the tribesmen. If he failed, there would be more than a thousand souls who would cry out against him at the final tribunal, and he would bear the weight of judgment.

Marelle was standing amidst the women, pale, holding too tightly onto her spear, but showing no fear in her expression. It was traditional for a general to give a speech before battle, to send the fire from his soul into the souls of his men. Radan Termith intended to kill Cete's wife. If even a fraction of the fire in Cete's soul went out to his men, they would burn.

Cete stood and faced his army. "You have come to the field of battle, though you have not been called," he said. "You have come to face a war from which you could have fled, without any shame. If this were a matter of honor, you would have already earned your share and more. There are few men who could stand in your place, and fewer women. You have come to fight, men and women, stonemasons and tanners, scholars and outcasts. If you wish to be proud, you have earned that right; if you wish to stand with honor among men of honor, none can deny you that place."

He was speaking as loud as he could, and the troops were quiet, but no more than a small fraction could hear him. They were . . . it was similar to the speech they had expected, and they were listening, trying to find within it a bit more courage than they had brought with them. Good enough; he'd give it to them if he could.

"This is not a matter of honor," he said. "This is a war.

This is a fight for your lives, for the lives of your families, for the lives of the children who cannot speak, and those too weak to stand. You are here to see that the Reach Antach will live, and that your homes will remain safe, and that you will beget children and grandchildren. We are fighting for everything; to stand in a place of honor is the smallest of the prizes for which we fight."

Cete had heard speeches made before battle a hundred times. He had made speeches himself, as a captain general of the Hainst. Where had he kept his hands, how had he kept the sweat from trickling down his face and into his eyes, how had he looked out at men who he hoped would stand their ground and die, rather than turn and run and live?

Earlier, during the morning services, he had planned out what he would say, but deciding was very different than doing. "Radan Termith is the captain general of the army of Reach Antach," he said. To hell with it. He would act, and if necessary, he would pay the price for his action. "The army of the Reach, and the militia of the Reach, are under his command. And under his command, they will buckle and flee when the enemy attacks."

That stilled the men. They had expected the usual sort of speech, with talk of honor and duty. Not this.

"The Termith is no traitor, outcast!" shouted someone from within the ranks.

"I did not suggest he was, Leran," said Cete. Radan's agent shrunk back—he had not expected to be identified. "And as you say, I am outcast. I am outcast because I stood and fought when he told me to run, because I was victorious, and thus showed his orders to be the orders of a coward."

Cete's audience did not know how to react. "Radan Termith is a coward," said Cete, louder than before. "And his fear will spread like a fever through his troops. You are not the fighting men who serve in the Reach army. You are not the trained militia lined up behind the army. But I tell you this—by standing here when you could flee, by taking up weapons when you could have remained within the walls, you have proved one thing to be true. None of you here are cowards!"

There was a sudden cheer at that. Cete took off his mantle, held it up before the men. "This is the finest thing that I have ever owned," he said. There was a faint patch of brown on the lining, where Marelle had cast it over his bleeding wounds. It was a flaw, an imperfection on something perfect, but it also fit. It made it his. He folded it, laid it on the ground, and pointed up to Marelle. "And that is the finest woman I have ever known. I am an outcast; I am past my prime as a fighting man. But I tell you this: Everything of value I have is here on this field. Come what may, I will not break, and I will not run. I ask from you nothing that I will not do myself. Stand, brave men, stand, true men, and when the charge comes upon you, break it with your spears!"

Another cheer, a louder one. It was not a standard speech, but it told them what they needed to hear.

"The law says," said Cete, and the crowd quieted, "that a man under arms must follow the orders of his superiors. There are exceptions. One of them is this: When an officer is in a rout, and is leading his troops in fleeing before the enemy, he and his men should be struck down by the sword, if they do not turn and fight, or withdraw in proper order."

No cheers at that, and neither did Cete expect any. "You have come here expecting to hold a line against tribesmen who come down from their lands seeking blood and plunder, and I tell you that you shall have to strike down your friends and neighbors, men of the Reach and men of the clans who support the Reach. It is a hard thing to hear, I know. But those men, when they are in the rout, they will be no less destructive than any tribesman. They will force open gates that need to be locked against enemies, they will lead our enemies into hidden places and refuges, they will bare your sons' breasts for the slaughter, and your daughters before the lust of the foe. A man in a rout is a wild beast, and he must not be allowed to roam the streets of the Reach!"

Still no cheering, but there was a hardening of faces, hands gripping tighter at their spears. "We will stand," said Cete. "For the law, for the right, and for Reach Antach!"

Cheers, then, and a relief in them. Perhaps this would put some iron in their spines, perhaps not. But now they knew what they needed to know. He went up and down the line, herding fifties into place, arranging his lines all along the terrace leading to the north gate. Down below, Radan made his final adjustments as well, and on the hilltops around, and down in the valley, lines of tribesmen began to draw up, each under their tribe's banner, each wearing the colors of their tribe.

The Antach clan army Cete arranged in a broad terrace, on his right flank. There was a steep slope down from that terrace. Poor footing, but one of the few routes where a charge could come without having to scale terraces, and down which a counterattack might be attempted, without the danger of climbing and leaping down from terrace to terrace. Kern Antach was there, at the head of his men, and wearing a high-plumed helm. He was not pleased.

"I've heard you called Radan a coward in front of your men," he said. "That was a foolish thing to do; it is an actionable thing to do, and you've given him yet another weapon."

"Mm," said Cete. "It is actionable now. I said that he would break and run, and I do not have sufficient proof to establish that claim, if he calls up a court. On the other hand, after he breaks and runs, it will be difficult for him to find a court that will hear with favor his claims, and levy any sanction. Even a court bought by the Termith will hesitate. There is no way they could rule against me without revealing their corruption."

"Then he will not break!" said Kern. "You are a captain general in the direct service of the Antach of the Antach. You speak with his voice, and your words are counted as his. He will stand, and he will break us in court more surely than on the field."

"And what of the tribes?" asked Cete. "Will they nod their heads at this strategy, call off their attack, and wait for the spoils to come to them through the courts of the law?"

Kern flicked his fingers. "He kills them, comes back in triumph, and your head, and my father's head decorate his standards. You've—"

"I would rather die with the Antach of the Antach than with the entire Reach Antach," said Cete. "But damning though it might be, the odds will not be so poor in a court as they are on this field. And besides, what happens the next time the Termith want the support of a tribe? Or other city clans, who are allied with the Termith? There are fourteen tribes who have sent their men against us, and they will never forget it if the plunder they have been promised turns into blood and ruin and a starvation winter. It's not just the tribes here that will learn of this treachery, and it is not just the tribes that are on this field who will revenge it."

Kern hesitated. "The Reach Antach, whole, is worth more than fidelity to sheep-thieves and rapists," he said. "But perhaps . . . but why did you do this? It is a grave risk, and an unnecessary one. You wouldn't have had to call him a coward if you waited for the rout; it would have been known without actionable speech."

"And what of my men?" asked Cete. "They are shopkeepers and miners, herdsmen and tree-pruners, women and outcasts. What would they think, when they see an army of fighting men break under the force of the tribes, when they see men with foam-flecked beards and open wounds come climbing up the terrace, pushing for the gate?"

Kern looked at Cete hard, as though he was trying to read truth and falsehood from his face, find the real reason why he had given so great an insult in a public speech. "Is it worth it?" he said. "To take such a risk, for the slight chance it will let this last line hold a moment longer?"

"It is my life," said Cete. "It is your life. It is my wife's life, it is your mother's life." He met Kern's gaze, just as serious as the young captain. "I am risking everything on the line holding, and you would be wise to do the same."

Kern swallowed, and just for the moment, Cete could see the boy in the captain general's clothing, see the fear and the hope and the sourness in the stomach that was a moment away from vomit. Cete clapped him on the shoulder. "I gave him an opportunity," said Cete. "But it's not one that he can take. The lines arranged by Radan Termith will break, and when a line of herdsmen and women holds where his army breaks, there'll be no hole deep enough for him to crawl into to hide his shame."

There was a moment of clarity in Kern's eyes. He would be the Antach after his father, if the clan still lived. "War's a risky business," said Kern. "We'd be better off without it."

Cete laughed. "Like it or not, we have it. Look to your men, and be ready for the charge."

"And you to yours," said Kern. He squared his shoulders, looked down into the valley. "Seems there'll be enough for everybody."

That there did. The skirmishers and slingers on either side were already circling around, trying to drive off their counterparts, find a weak place in their opponent's formations. Cete made his way back to his standard, took up his position a few paces in front of his banner and his folded mantle. He'd rather trust to his axe and dagger than to a spear; should the line collapse, he would not be able to bring a spear to bear before being overwhelmed. He had chosen the weakest fifty to stand by his sides, to be firmed up by the general's standard, and by the example he would set. So he set that example, holding his spear ready, facing the foe.

The skirmishing did not take long. The first line of the tribesmen charged forward, and were repulsed by the lines of the Reach, leaving dead strewn across the field. That line had flown banners of all the tribes who had come to lay siege on Reach Antach, a tithe of slain to make it seem as though Radan Termith was a defender of the Reach, rather than a more deadly foe than any tribal chieftain.

Then the horns blew and the drums pounded, and even up on the hill, before the gates of the Reach, the ghastly wail of the tribal battlecry caused men to flinch, step back, let the points of their spears go up. "Hold," roared Cete, and all along the line his fifty-commanders echoed his command. "Ready!"

There was the clash of steel on steel, of iron on brass, and Radan's lines buckled under the press of the tribesmen. It seemed he did not intend to take the opportunity that Kern Antach had seen. The center of the line fell in, and the flanks pulled up, and then the army of the Reach broke and ran.

For a moment, it looked as though the militia might hold. Their horns blew the charge, their commanders tried to keep their men in formation, tried to staunch the holes that had sprung up in the lines of the Reach Army. There was no way. The force of men was too great, and there were traitors in the militia's ranks as well.

The slaughter was well begun. The men of the Reach army had been spared the worst of the tribal assault. Men fell, here and there, to javelin and slung shot, to tribal warriors who forgot secret treaties and alliances when faced with the undefended back of a man of a reach. But the militia were not spared, and they fell as they fled, gasping, climbing up through terraces, past trees and through gardens, minds lost to fear.

The line near the gate wavered. Cete's men had taken up weapons because they thought they wanted to fight, but they were not so certain when faced with the real thing. "Hold!" roared out Cete, again. "Lower spears!"

They wavered, but they held, the spearpoints coming down in their ranks. A row of points four feet from the first line, and a second one coming between their shoulders, the men in the second rank ready to strike out against any who crossed the first line of spears. "I've stood in the line," said Cete, loud enough to be heard over the frightened mutters of his men. "And I've joined in the flight when we were routed. If you but hold, if you turn back the first wave of the rout, men will awaken from their fever and sickness. They will take up arms beside you, they will fill any gaps that others have made. Hold fast, my brothers and sisters. Hold fast, and live!"

The men of the Reach army outpaced the militia. They were fleeter of foot, and they ran to a purpose, rather than in blind fear. As Cete had intended, the easiest path led up to where the Antach clan army was waiting, and men who came up that way fell back, wounded and dying. Militia men and men of the Reach army died at the hands of their lord's clan, as the horns blew "hold fast," and the officers barked at them to turn and fight.

Then the trickle became a wave, and all along the line, men of the Reach fought men of the Reach, as their enemies climbed up the terraces below, making ready to kill. The line held. Shopkeepers brought down veterans, farmers killed sergeants. A spear thicket is a deadly thing, if it holds, and this one held.

Held, and bled. Here and there a group of soldiers pushed past the line of points, and slew, axes, and swords making short work of men in leather cloaks, of women in homemade armor. Each time it happened, the second rank became the first, and the third became the second, not letting them come through in sufficient numbers to break the line. Here and there, militia men caught hold of themselves, chose between the fear of death at their backs and the certainty of death if they pressed forward, and turned to face the tribesmen, who were already climbing up to meet them.

In the center of the line, where Cete stood with his men, the push was as bloody as anywhere. Of the fifty command he had led into battle, forty-seven men had died in battle or of their wounds, or had marched out with Radan. The three who remained—Canien, Mata, and Alband—he'd kept by his side. Canien stood at his left, and was killed by a flung axe, and Mata cut down by a swordsman who came in with a spear in his side, madness in his eyes, and spittle in his beard. But Alband came up and took Mata's place, and the line held.

Cete's fighters held all along the line. Shopkeepers took the places of silver merchants, fig-cutters the places of shopkeepers. After a time, even the men of the Reach army came to understand that they would not be allowed to flee into the Reach, they would not be allowed to take their traitor's pay, and walk away with the loot of the Reach. They drew up in their ranks below the spear thicket, tried to find a path around, huddled and stopped, sheep confronted by a fence.

A captain of the army came forward to where Cete's standard stood. "By order of Radan Termith, Captain General of Reach Antach, let us pass; we are needed on the wall."

"You are needed in the field," replied Cete. "Stand and fight, or be slain as a coward."

"You have no authority," said the captain. He turned away from Cete, towards the men who stood at his left. "The walls are life, and this man is death," he said. "Go back now, while there is time, and the walls will be manned. If you obey an outcast and scorn the words of your rightful commander, you will die and be damned for it; if you—"

Cete leapt from the ranks. One of the captain's men tried to intercept him, and Cete's elbow caught him below the chin, sent him backwards off of the terrace. The captain turned as Cete came on, fumbling for his axe. Cete grabbed him, pulled him down. "You can't," started the captain. "My orders—"

One stroke with the axe, and the spray of blood. Another, and the captain's body fell to the earth. His face wore a look of astonishment; he had expected to kill that day, not to be killed.

There was horror on the face of the men who had seen what Cete had done. His men, and the men of the Reach army. Damn them all. "Radan Termith is the captain general of the Reach Antach," roared out Cete. "He has authority over its defense. But I will not accept disobedience from his lieutenants, from cowards who fled a fight that could be won."

He turned out towards the tribal army that was advancing, rising up from terrace to terrace, coming up like a swarm of ants towards a pile of fallen grain. He drew back his arm, and threw the captain's head in a great, bloody arc, to bounce down towards the oncoming horde. "Fight or die," he said. Again, louder. "Fight or die! You will not hide behind the backs of men and women who retain their honor!"

The remainder of that captain's fifty looked towards Cete, and then back down to the oncoming tribesmen. They had expected—they had been promised—treachery and plunder, the rewards of service to the Termith against the upstart Antach. Now, they knew what every soldier learns; they knew that they would die. They could fight for the Reach, if they chose. They would be in the front rank, and many had left their weapons behind as they ran.

Others, elsewhere along the line, joined with the defenders Cete had raised. Militia men, for the most part, who took up spears, who filled holes that had been made by their rout. Men of the Reach army as well, though Cete had given orders to his fifty-commanders that they were not to be allowed into the ranks. It was to be expected; he had made officers almost randomly, and some of them were not suited for command, not willing to make sacrifices when giving way would be easier.

Hopefully, those would not do too much damage. The majority of the Reach army was held back, forced to stand in front of the spear thicket. There were good men who Cete was dooming with those orders, men whose only fault was in officers they had not chosen, and in orders they could not disobey. But most of the good men in the Reach army were already dead, killed in Radan's other engagements with the tribal coalition, or taken into slavery. The men who milled about beyond the spear thicket were mostly Termith aligned, and they knew how the battle was supposed to go.

Groups of them threw down their weapons, and advanced down the slope with open hands. Cete smiled grimly at that. The Termith were afraid that if the Reaches were to find an accommodation with the tribes, it would weaken the hold of the city clans. They still might extinguish that danger in the ashes of Reach Antach. But if anyone survived who had seen this battle, tribesman or reachman, the Termith might find themselves wishing they could brag of their treachery, to drown out the reputation for cowardice their treachery had earned. If people discounted the strength of the Termith, if they refused to take contracts from Termith-aligned fighting men, their clan was in a position little better than the Antach.

It was a victory, but a costly one, and not one that gave much aid against the oncoming tribesmen, who climbed up through the terraces like coils of snakes, like smoke rising through a pile of wood. Here and there, they met with patches of surrendering soldiers from the Reach army, with men of the militia who were too injured to climb up the whole way to the walls. Some of them lived to be taken captive, but most were cut down where they stood. There was blood in the air, and the plunder of a wealthy reach. The killing fever had come, and no secret alliance would be strong enough to hold it back.

There were too many tribesmen. If all his troops were fighting men, and if the walls were defended with bow and javelin, they could have been driven off. But they were not, and they were not, and the Termith and their allies had spent a fortune raising up their tribal army. The enemy would be tired from the climb, they would be coming up on a readied defense where they expected helpless meat, but there were too many. Cete's lines could not save the Reach Antach.

He knew it, but his men did not. They had fought their first battle, and they had won. And they knew that tribesmen were worse fighters than civilized men, they knew that they had the law on their side, and the walls of their homes to protect. They steeled themselves, moved their spears into position.

The line of men was drawn up near the base of a ter-race wall, and the line of women and children and others who had come to fight without being mustered waited at the base of the next terrace up. Marelle stood among the women, a smudge of dirt on her cheek, her spear unbloodied, her neighbors by her sides. If the wall fifty tried to break Cete's line with missiles, the terraces would shield them. But that wasn't the limit of the mischief that they could cause, and as the tribes came forward, he sent a runner to the Antach clan army—hold back as well you can, and look to the rear.

It was time. Cete gave the order, and the slingers and men with javelins came through the ranks, and began their work. There were only fifty of them, and the terraces and trees provided good cover. One tribesman fell, an-other, a grain of dirt in the avalanche that was coming up the hill. Still, one less enemy left alive to enjoy the plun-der, one less tribesman who would count himself lucky to have come to the walls of the Reach Antach.

Then the slingers retreated back through the ranks, and the men who had flung their javelins took up spears, for the enemy was upon them. The previous attack had come in dribs and drabs; a squad here, a fifty-command there, all disordered, some too maddened with fear to see the spears that killed them. The tribesmen came in good order, their wails rising up to the heavens, and they hit all along the line at once.

It buckled. They were forced back a foot, then another. All along the line, his men killed, but the tribesmen came up over the bodies of their slain, more, always more. Another foot, and Cete could see gaps starting to show in the ranks to his left, between his position and where he had stationed his fifties of sword and axe.

Buckled, but held. Women came down to fill the gaps where men had fallen. Men from the Reach army held out in their hopeless clusters, men who had forgotten everything of plot and plan and knew only that their enemies were upon them with sword and axe and tribal chant.

For a long time they sweated there in the noonday sun, exhausted and terrified men against exhausted and terrified men. If they could not take the Reach, half the tribes that had mustered up against it would not survive the winter. Too few hands to do the work, too few young men to protect their sheep and grain from those who had not marched in the summer. It was fight or die, fight and die, on both sides.

It was a glorious defense, but it could not last. There were too few defenders, too untrained, and while the women fought with valor, they tired quickly, unaccustomed to the weight of weapons. Another step back, and Cete's foot touched the mantle he had left folded on the ground. He would not go farther back; if the men at his sides retreated, he would die where he stood. Marelle was behind him, between two of her friends. She would fall soon after him, as she had wished.

Off in the distance, there was the sound of a tribal horn, little different from those that were sounding out the orders in the field before him. Perhaps . . . it was a hope born of desperation, but it was what he had. Cete set his own horn to his lips, and blew the charge.

It echoed along the line, horns held up to bruised, astonished lips, and men awoke to its sound, pushing forward against the line which had been pushing them back for what seemed like their entire lives. Legs unlocked from defensive poses, spears were lowered, and they stepped forward. One step, another. This was the last of the reserves they had. If the tribesmen rallied, the line would not again hold.

A third step, a fourth. Cete nearly tripped over Alband's body; the last of his fifty, and Cete had not seen him fall. Forward, more, beyond where the lines had stood. The tribesmen fell back, surprised. They had expected easy meat, and fine things taken from a burning reach. They knew as well as Cete that these were not fighting men who opposed them. It could not last; they would rally, and his line would be crushed.

The main line could not sustain a push, let alone a

charge. But on the flanks, there were the fifties of axe and sword to the left, and the Antach clan army to the right. There, they took one terrace, and then another. The tribes in the center wavered. If they pushed back, they might reach the gates of the Reach, might have the treasure they were promised. But if they could not break through, they would be encircled, killed like sheep in the springtime, when the shepherds make their cull.

A cheer came up, along the line. One terrace, two. The tribesmen showed their heels. Those who did not run were slain, and some of those who did run could not outpace the spears that followed them. They bled too, they feared too, they too called out in anguish from the dirt, and did not rise again.

A third terrace. Cete looked back, and there was a fifty marching out from the gate, the banners of the Reach army floating over their ranks. The Antach clan army was two terraces down, killing well, but with no men left behind to secure the rear. He blew the halt, and it was not heeded. Blew again, louder, giving everything to it. A few of the men remembered enough of their discipline to come to a stop, a few others picked up the call, and the lines of spear gradually re-formed, as the chance they saw vanished, the tribesmen flying down into the valley below.

Chapter 11

This was a test of discipline that Cete had never anticipated giving his troops, and would never have expected
them to pass. To maintain discipline when at grips was
difficult. To maintain it in the face of defeat, when the
troops were sure they would die if they stood, and live
if they fled, that was more difficult. But to follow orders
in the face of triumph, to allow cold reason to douse the
flames of glory—there were veteran troops who would
not have obeyed the order Cete had given.

But there was no time for pride in the accomplish-
ments of his army. Cete turned, leapt up a terrace wall
into the ranks of women and children who had been following. There was confusion, and he had to swat aside a
spear to get to the rear of his army before the fifty-command fell on their backs.

But the men who had come down from the wall did
not come with weapons bared. Mase was at their head,
and he bowed to Cete as he came forward. "It seems the
Reach army is lost," said Mase. "And you are the captain
general of the Antach. We wish to volunteer our service."

"These are not the orders you've been given, Fifty-Commander Mase," said Cete, cautiously, his hand still on his axe. "Should I accept your service, I would fear for your safety in a court of law."

There was a long pause, as Mase seemed to look for words to say, and Cete for reasons to believe. "Army's all I know, Cete," said Mase. "Radan Termith isn't going to be repeating his orders in a court of law, you can believe that. But the Termith won't back up what he did say, not for a mess like this. Not with money, not with anything."

He shrugged, looked around at Cete's army, at the tribesmen making their way down to their camp. "I tried to warn you off," he said. "It was all arranged by then. No need to add another damn fool corpse to the pile. But you fought, and damn if you didn't wreck everything they'd planned. It's all gone to hell. Maybe not for Radan, but for everyone who swore the liar's oaths on his behalf. Army is all I know, and you've made a line worth dying on."

Cete let go his axe, pulled close the man who had scarred him for disobedience to orders, wept on the shoulder of the man who had beaten him near to death. "Good and well," he said. "You come in good time."

He turned back to the men who waited for his orders. "Back up to the wall," he said.

"Not the wall," said Mase. "The captain of the Reach

army may still live. He, and his chief engineer. There are weak places known only to them; if the tribesmen come up against the wall, it will not slow them."

Cete blew "re-form lines" on his horn, and the command was echoed all along the line. His army of bakers and shopkeepers marched back up the narrow stairways of the terraces in good order, as the tribesmen formed up below. If he had not stopped then, regardless of the wall fifty, the battle would have been lost on those lower terraces. The men had been spreading out in their pursuit, the fast outstripping the slow. When the tribesmen turned on them, it would have been a slaughter.

If the wall had not been undermined, they would have been able to hold. That it had been undermined meant that the only reason the tribes were coming after them rather than making for the weak points of the wall was because they did not wish to start the plunder while an organized troop still opposed them. Scatter the men across a weakened wall, and the battle was already lost.

At the base of the wall, the men and women took their rest, took long draughts of water and wine, tied cloth over wounds they had not noticed in the heat of battle. Some had left, wounded or heartsick or simply unable to continue, and more had died. It was a smaller company by far than that which had started the day below the walls of the Reach Antach.

Marelle was with them. A friend had died on her shoulder; there was blood on her leather coat, and pain on her face, but she still intended to stand and fight, and still had the strength to hold her spear. Cete looked down at the tribesmen in the valley. There were fewer of them as well, and while they were no longer fleeing, they were slow in arranging their lines. Another two hundred men, and he could have smashed them, ended the threat to the Reach in the blood of its enemies.

He didn't have two hundred more men. He did not have nearly as many men as he needed. Cete turned to arranging his own lines. The fifty of sling and javelin had become ten slingers, whose arms ached with constant effort. The three fifties of sword and axe he had set on his left flank had become a single fifty-command, and of the nine fifties of spearmen, there were four remaining, each of them a patchwork of men from the militia and from the Reach army and from those who had come to Cete's call. Added to that was another fifty of women of the Reach; there had been four times that number at the start of the battle, but most had left with wounds, or carrying off the wounded. He could have used them back on the field, but he could not fault them for leaving. It had been the sort of field that even ten-year veterans would be glad to leave, if they could. Marelle was among the women, a neighbor at her side. Cete did not go to her, because if he had, he would have asked her to leave the field, and by her pained look, she might have. It would not be right for him to take strength away from her, not even to save her life.

The Antach clan army had not fared so poorly; they had started with five fifties, and five banners still flew beneath the Antach clan's crest. Not that they were full fifties—they had lost perhaps half the strength they had started with—but the organization remained.

It was no longer possible to leave the ends of the line strong enough to mount a charge. Cete arranged his troops on a higher terrace than he had before, in shorter lines. The Antach's men were in the center, with the wall fifty on the right flank, and Cete to the left, with the rest of the units stringing between, men and women together, arrayed in three lines; a two-line spear hedge, a third line to fill in the gaps, and the fifty of axe and sword as the only reserve.

Cete picked up his mantle, shook the dust from its hem, and folded it again. It had been trampled in the back and forth of battle, but it was still whole and perfect. The tribesmen below were forming up into lines, each man to the flag of his tribe. No longer bound by the will of the city clans, they had to decide if they wanted to attempt the Reach again. The conclusion was fore-ordained. There was too small a force protecting too great a treasure, and they had lost too much in the attempt to leave the plunder and their dead behind. But all the voices would be heard, and rivalries would force argument even when logic called for an immediate march.

Again, the distant voice of strange horns. It was too much to hope, so Cete put it from his mind. They would hold against one more charge. Maybe two; they were men who had been tested, who had stood against a horde three times their own numbers, and who had not broken. They might not be veterans, but they knew who they were, and what they faced.

As the tribesmen formed up into lines and made ready to attempt the Reach again, a few more men came out from the gates of the Reach Antach, among them the Antach himself. He found Cete where he stood in the line, laid an arm across his shoulders. "You have done more than was possible," he said. "And it seems that you shall earn rewards similar to those your service to me has earned you in the past."

Cete turned his head away. "I have no complaints," he said. "Though it is possible that my contract is a little light."

The Antach laughed. "Perhaps," he said. "But one does not become the head of a clan by paying more than the seller requires. It is to be hoped that next year, you shall require more, and I shall have more to spend."

Below, the drums began again, and the horns. They were ready. "They will come soon, Lord," said Cete. "Perhaps you should—"

"I cannot stand at the head of the army of my clan," said the Antach, "according to the terms of my contract with the Termith."

"Does that still matter?" asked Cete.

"It may," replied the Antach. "There have been no messengers from my brother, and none of the men who I have sent out have returned. But I have not yet given up hope."

"Of course," said Cete. Hope was all the Antach had left, and he would not leave it behind unless forced.

"As I was saying, I cannot stand with my own sworn men. But there is nothing in the contract that forbids me from taking up an axe with the volunteers, and doing the work of a fighting man. I would put myself under your orders, captain general, if you will have me."

Cete bowed. "Can you have any rank, or—"

"None," said the Antach. "Not even a sergeant's."

If the tribes did not take the Reach, but the Antach was killed, he did not know how Kern would react. Once the fighting was over, he would need the favor of the nobles of the Reach to stay alive, and either denying the Antach his request or granting it could imperil that.

"The fifty of axe and sword are a reserve," he said. "If

you would join them, they could use the aid of a man trained for war." There was no policy in that, no calculation. The man wanted to fight, and that was where he was most needed. He would live or die depending on the fortunes of battle, his skill in arms, and upon the will of God, the same as any man on the line.

The Antach saluted and headed to his station, and Cete turned to watch the tribesmen come up the hill, clambering up terrace walls, axes slung behind their backs, knives held in their teeth. They were a terrible sight, and he could feel the tension all along the line; muscles tensing, the fear clenching stomachs. He could see lips and knuckles going white, men and women looking as though they were about to vomit, or faint.

"Steady!" yelled Cete. Then he started singing the battle hymn. They were not fighting men, most of them, and they had never heard the hymn sung with readied weapons, on a field that was stained and splotched with blood. Enough knew the hymn that the chorus carried through, and though the words were sometimes broken, they all could feel its power.

It worked. It worked so well that the lines took two steps forward when the tribesmen came to grips. Forward, by God, though by all rights they should have broken. The wave of tribesmen was pushed back to the edge of the terrace and beyond, pushed over the edge onto those still climbing, so that they all fell below, breaking bones and necks. A step back, as the tribesmen came up again, and another step forward, pushing them back again.

Again and again, the wave of the tribes lapped against the weapons of the men of the city, and again and again, they were forced back in blood and anguish. It could not last. It didn't. The tribesmen carved out for themselves beachheads, flowed up where their footing was secure. Gaps appeared in the spear thicket, gaps which pushed back against the reserves which tried to fill them.

The man at Cete's left fell to a tribal sword, flat-bladed and wide, and the man who stepped up to replace him fell soon after. Then, nobody stepped to fill the gap, and Cete left his spear behind, switching to his axe and his hook-bladed tribal knife. He killed, killed again, and was forced back, back to where his mantle lay folded on the blood-speckled grass. Marelle was there, still fighting, and he found himself in the ranks beside her.

For all that she was blind, it was good to fight by her side. She kept her spear point forward, as he had taught her, using it to feel for targets, and striking out with flurries which seldom hit, but which forced her opponents to step back, to guard against her rather than strike her down.

The doctor who had sewn up Cete's back, after Mase

had cut it open, rolled up against Cete's leg, her face loose in death, her uncalloused hands red with blood. The press of men beyond was too great for Cete to push the corpse off him, and if he took another step back, the mantle would be lost. He braced himself, struck out against the tribesman who was hounding him, and took a cut across the forehead in exchange. Not enough to break the bone, but there was blood there, coming down into his eyes. Another cut. This time, Cete anticipated, got in underneath the tribesman, jabbed his knife into the man's eye before he could bring his sword down.

They fell together, the tribesman trying to recover until Cete forced the knife in deeper, pressing against the hilt with the palm of his hand, until the tribesman convulsed, stiffened, and then was still. Another man came over them, where they lay together. Marelle's side was undefended, and she could not see the axe swinging into her side.

Cete rose up from beneath the corpse, caught the man by groin and neck, so that the blow merely glanced off Marelle's ribs, rather than cutting through leather coat, meat and bone. Cete lifted him and threw him up and over, back into the press of tribesmen. His spear was abandoned; the knife would not come out from where he had left it, and his axe was pinned beneath the dead tribesman. Marelle wore a knife at her belt. Cete grabbed it, turned like a cat, ready to strike out. It wasn't a fighting knife; the blade would snap at the least resistance. But if it would find a throat, it would be enough, and it was what he had.

Just then, there was confusion in the tribal ranks, and horns rang out the charge from their rear. Horns and drums, and the sounds of slaughter. Cete lifted his horn to his lips and blew out the charge, and again the men of the Reach responded, coming forward, weapons lowered.

Again, the tribesmen started back, but this time it was not merely giving way in the face of a foe who showed unexpected strength. They were assailed from the rear, and they knew it, and this time, their rout was complete. It gave enough space for Cete to find his axe, to see that Marelle's wound was not mortal. Then he was leaping forward in pursuit, catching tribesmen from behind and leaving them dead, like a leopard leaping from the back of one sheep to the next, killing and killing again, as the White Horn tribe, the tribe of the Antach's brother, came up the valley, sweeping aside anything that lay in their path.

Again the charge, the hunting charge, knowing that the tribesmen would not be able to turn at bay, paying back in kind and more every death since the day by that dry riverbed. The Antach clan army came down the hill as well, their armor golden and terrible in the sun, and running among them were men of the Reach, who had not lived as fighting men, but who had become fighting men when the need of their homes was upon them. It was a glory like unmixed wine, like the sun when it touches the peaks of the mountains, like the first rains of winter on a dry and hungry land.

It was not long before they broke into small groups, as the tribesmen bounded away this way and that, forgetting all order and claims of brotherhood in their panic. Thus, Cete was alone when he came upon Radan Termith, alive amidst the ruins of the tribal camp, where the long-awaited rescue had broken them like a dropped jar.

He was wearing his hair up in victory braids, and he had a breastplate painted over in ochre and white. For those who did not know him, he would have been just another tribal warrior. But Cete knew him. It was Radan Termith, whole, with an axe in his hands. Cete felt his heart rise up in his chest, the boil of his blood opening the cuts he had taken that morning. "A good day, captain general," said Cete.

Radan gave a hoarse laugh. He was alive, but he was not unmarked. There was a cut on his left arm, a jagged thing with clots of blood hanging to the tight curled hair of his arm, and there was a hesitation in his right leg. He circled, crabwise, and Cete matched his movements. He reached out with the axe, a short blow, just to test Cete's defense, but Cete's axe was so hungry for blood, he had to fight back the urge to take that bait, fight back the inclination to end it in a single pass.

"A good day, captain general," replied Radan, still circling. "It seems the field is yours."

Cete smiled, slowly. "Not yet. There are still men living who came up against the Reach Antach."

Radan's smile matched his. "Be a long, long time before you'll claim that. Long after the name Antach is forgotten."

"Perhaps," said Cete. He came forward. The limp was feigned, and he proved that—Radan moved quickly enough, when it was that or have his side cut. But the weariness was not, nor the weakness in his left arm. Cete had taken hurts as well, was tired as well. But it was not enough to make up the difference; Radan Termith would lose.

Radan saw that too, paled. "Quarter!" he cried.

"No," said Cete, still circling.

"The law says you must—"

"A man who leads a congregation astray," said Cete, "is a public menace, akin to a wolf or hyena that has come within the walls of a city. He shall be struck down, and also his family shall bear the sin."

"Damn you!" Radan shook his head, tried to clear it. "This is the will of the Termith of the Termith, the Hainst of the Hainst, the Coardur of the Coardur! I've led nothing; I've followed, and more will follow."

"More will follow," echoed Cete. "And follow further down your road as well."

Radan tried again, driving forward. Cete gave him ground, clipped the side of his head with his axe. Not deep enough to cut bone, but enough to peel back a strip of flesh, send blood down his neck and side.

"The Antach," said Radan. "He'll want me alive. This is his chance, to have something to bargain with. Kill me, and risk the future of the Reach. The Antach will want me alive, the Termith will want me alive. Give quarter, and you'll be rewarded by both—you and your wife will have a place with the Antach so long as they live, and the Termith when they fail."

It was true that the Antach would like Radan Termith alive, and confessing his treachery. And it was true that he was a son of the Termith, and for all that he had failed, they would not wish to see him dead on the battlefield, his bones scattered in a strange land. Cete pulled back, out of range; damned if he'd let Radan take an advantage while he thought. And rational thought all pointed in one direction.

"If the Antach of the Antach wished for me to spare

you," he said, "he ought to have paid me more."

Radan tried to say something else, but then the madding had Cete, a rage so vast he could not contain it. He came in, Radan's axe came up, faster than Cete had expected. Not fast enough. He took Radan's throat out with Marelle's knife, and as the former captain general fell and choked, his axe went through the man's chest, cutting through armor and muscle and bone to lay open his heart.

It was done. Cete threw back his head, and a roar tore from his own heart, as open as the ruin of Radan's. It was better to live than to die, and for the heaps and rows of those slain by the gate of the Reach Antach, he could not suffer Radan Termith to live, no matter the politics or the cost. Rational thought pointed in one direction, but it was not a road down which Cete could travel. It was done, and it was well done, and it was over.

Chapter 12

The Antach and his brother met on the field, after the fighting was done, and embraced each other. The men of the tribe came up into the Reach for the feasting, and the survivors of the battle were made welcome in the tents of the White Horn tribe, and in the tents of their allies pitched in the valley below, and up on the hills. All those slain of the Reach Antach—militia and clan army and Reach army, those who fought with honor and those who had attempted to bathe in blood the Reach who owned their service—were laid to rest in the graveyard just outside the walls of the Reach Antach. There is no treachery in death, there is no honor, just the long silence of the underworld, and the judgment of the true judge.

There were a great many dead. Cete stood beside the Antach at every burial, said a blessing for the names of all the slain whose names were known, gave over to God those names which were not known. Tarreer was dead, as was Arthran, the boy from the gauntlet. He had fought with the wall fifty, and his face looked even younger in death, his nose still crooked from Cete's punch.

When the slain were buried and the wounds of those who lived were treated by the doctor's apprentices, Cete retreated back to his house on the outskirts of town, back to Marelle. They had to tend to their trees before the harvest, and had to consider what would be done with the bare patch of land he had purchased during his long battle with Radan Termith. Cete was still the captain general of the Reach Antach, but it would be some time before that title had much meaning. The Reach army numbered eighty men hale enough to be called up to fight, with another hundred in the militia.

For the time, the defense was left to the Antach's brother and his White Horn tribe, and the allies that had followed the White Horn banner. It was a tribe with a celebrated lineage, and hunting grounds extending far to the north and northeast. The delay the Termith had thrown at them had been entirely to their benefit—they had hit an army that was already uncertain and weary, and had earned a great harvest of plunder and slaves, at relatively little cost. That would bind the tribal allies to them, in the same way that what had passed before the walls of Reach Antach would cause tribes to fear any contact with the Termith. If the Reach Antach was still perched on perilous ground, the future of the White Horns seemed secure, at least for the season.

They were certainly strong enough to protect the

Reach, or to sack it, regardless of what Cete did. So he appointed fifty-commanders and sergeants, and left them to rebuild the army as best they could; he signed the contracts, he took responsibility for the men they hired on, but he did not oversee their training, nor did he seek out volunteers, nor train men up for work with spears. For a week, he saw to raising monuments over the burials, and worked with the Antach's men to make sure that all those who sought the gifts given to the bereaved had legitimate claims.

Marelle had her commissions to attend to. And there were some small tears in the sunset mantle; while she appreciated the nature of Cete's gesture, it required careful work to repair what he had damaged. When she could, she helped with the work in the orchards, or gave Cete advice about the men in the army. But there were times when she would sit with a haunted look, her hand on the shoulder where her friend's blood had been spilled. The cut with the axe was not the only blow she had taken on the field that day, nor even the one that pained her most.

One evening, when the sun had not yet set, but the heat of the day had faded, the Antach's men came up around the orchard, as they had the night that he had been made captain general, and once again, the Antach was in the field waiting, with his son at one side, and Lemist Irimin on the other. Cete bowed, took up the chair which had been made ready for him.

There was some casual talk, before any business was mentioned. The Antach inquired after Marelle, Kern complimented Cete on the rebuilding of the Reach army, and the steps he had taken to probe the Reach walls for weakness, and to repair the damage that they had undergone during the administration of Radan Termith. Cete replied with compliments for the Antach clan army, for the valor and timely arrival of the White Horn tribe.

When that was done, the Antach leaned back. "I have not had a chance to properly congratulate you on your victory. Were it not for the minor observances of mourning between Summer Candles and the Festival of Sheaves, I would have called a feast in your honor, and sent presents to you and your wife. It was a victory unlooked for, and your name is now heard upon the lips of the mighty men of the cities."

Cete winced slightly at that last. Those mighty men of the cities—"the Termith of the Termith, the Hainst of the Hainst, the Coardur of the Coardur"—were the ones Radan had named as the men who had sought the destruction of the Reach Antach. While his name was certainly heard from their lips, it would not be surrounded by praise of his work, or prayers for his continued success. "It's not just the minor observances of mourning that hold you back," he said.

"No," said Lemist. "The orders you had been given were wrong, but they were not criminal. Besides, a court has ruled on this issue, and there is no evidence that corruption or bribes changed the result. You are outcast, and you shall remain outcast. A feast might be given in your honor, but you would not be permitted to sit at the tables with the men of the Reach."

"It would be peculiar," said Cete, "for me to sit outside the gates, and ask for scraps from the feast, amidst the other outcasts."

"Peculiar," said the Antach. "But within the law. All honor that can be done for you within the law shall be done."

"Thank you," said Cete, and waited.

"It is a difficult thing which I have come to ask you," said the Antach.

"You wish to buy back the remainder of my contract," said Cete. The simplest thing for the Antach of the Antach to do would have been to have arranged for Cete's murder, but there were risks involved in that. This would be more honorable, and safer, and Cete had expected it from the moment he stood over the lifeless corpse of Radan Termith, and watched the last of the tribesmen flee into the hills.

"They have already reached you?" asked the Antach. "I would have expected more caution on the part of the city clans, but I suppose it would be well for them to act quickly."

Cete hesitated, tried to fit things into place, and could not. "I am sorry," he said. "I do not understand."

"I feel it is the Termith who have the fullest under-standing of what happened here," said the Antach, "for reasons that I shall not discuss, lest I inadvertently slan-der an ancient and honorable clan. But the other city clans have watched what transpired with a keen interest as well. There are men coming to the Reach Antach who will seek you out over the next few days and weeks, of-fering to buy your labor at rates much higher than those which I am able to pay."

Cete was silent, stunned, hands lifeless on the arms of his chair. He had set himself against the Termith when he forced Radan to brand him as an outcast, and he had counted them as his enemy ever since.

"If a man owns racing pigeons," said the Antach, kindly, "and a rival he had not considered worthy of at-tention flies a bird that outpaces all of his, his first instinct is not to cut that bird's throat, Cete. They will seek to buy you, and with offers that are not mere silver."

He had been thinking like a fighting man, and not like the lord of a clan. The Antach was right. The Termith of the Termith would resent that his plan was foiled, but Cete was no more his enemy than his own hook-bladed tribal knife was Cete's mortal foe.

"They will promise you doctors who will restore Marelle's sight, and they will promise you a new trial, with witnesses who will swear that the orders you heard were not legitimately given, that two of the three judges in your previous trial had not judged honestly. And perhaps they will deliver on these promises. More than that, they will offer you something that I assuredly cannot. They will promise you long life, far from the field of battle, a safe place where you can raise up sons and daughters, and that your name will live through them."

From within his mantle, the Antach pulled forth a small pouch, and tossed it to Cete. There was the weight and sound of silver. "One quarter of the value remaining in your contract," said the Antach. "You are free of the contract between us, your duties discharged in a satisfactory fashion. I owe you too much to stand in your way. If you choose to leave, go in good health, and with my blessing."

"I take it, then, that you wish to offer me another choice," said Cete, fighting for his balance.

"I do," said the Antach. "The mines of the Reach Antach have done well, and as of the festival of Sheaves, we will have paid off the founding debt and all the interest that we owe to the city clans." This was an astounding bit of news. The Reach Antach had been founded in living memory; Reach Tever had stood for three hundred years, and owed a debt greater than the cost of its founding.

"Accordingly, I do not have the silver to pay you what your labor is worth, or even to match the offers that the city clans will make. Furthermore, I cannot promise you a doctor who can restore sight to the blind, or a court who will take in what another has cast out."

"It was a fair trial," said Lemist. "And the verdict was in accordance with the law."

The Antach gave a short nod at that. "More, and worse, the Reach Antach is not so safe a place, as you have seen. And when a pigeon racer cannot acquire a rival's birds, there is the ferret and the hawk and poison in the mash. There are a great many reasons why you should not take the offer I shall make, and I will not fault you for hearing the voice of those reasons."

Cete felt a tension within him. The Antach of the Antach knew him well; what he had said, and how he had said it made Cete wish to take up the offer, whatever it was. But those were good reasons, and he ought to listen to them.

"If you would fight with us, continue on as my captain general, there will be no further need of contracts between us. You would be adopted into the Antach, to share in our fortune, to eat the meat from our table, and your voice would be heard in the councils of our family."

It was as sudden and as hard as a well-struck blow from an axe. To bear the name of the clan—for a city clan like the Hainst or the Termith, there would be hundreds of men and women in the family. The Antach were a young clan. There were not yet cousin lines and second-cousin lines or any of the endless branches of a well-established dynasty. "How many . . ." Cete trailed off.

"You would be eighth in line," said the Antach. "After my sons, and four of my cousins."

"Too high," said Cete. "Too much of a risk of an outcast Antach."

"That would be a disaster, and no question," said Kern. "Death of the clan, as likely as not. But it is necessary, to secure your children a place among the family lines of the first rank."

"I—" started Cete.

"No," said the Antach. "Not tonight. There is no contract, but this cannot be decided on an impulse, in the dark. Tomorrow, after the morning services, come to me and tell me what you have decided. If you are with me, it must be with your whole soul. I will not have you resentful, I will not have you feeling as though I tricked you into making a poor choice. As Radan Termith has taught us, the Reach Antach cannot trust a captain general of uncertain loyalties."

"Thank you," said Cete, and bowed deeply. The Antach stood and bowed to Cete, as did Kern, as did Lemist, and then they left into the night, with their men formed up around them. Cete went back into his house, and though Marelle waited on the roof, he remained below.

After a time, Marelle made her careful way down the ladder, with a hitch, where her side still pained her. She came over to where he was sitting, though he had said nothing, and put her hand upon his shoulder. He started at her touch, as though he had been awakened from a dream.

"You have your mantle out," she said.

"Yes," said Cete. "And the shroud you have embroidered for me. I have a choice to make."

"Tell me," she said, and he told her.

When he was done, she was silent for a long time. "It is your labor," she said. "It must be your choice."

"No," said Cete. "It is my labor, but it is your life, and it is the life of our children yet unborn. Perhaps for myself I would choose the shroud, but I cannot choose it for you as well."

"If you choose the Hainst or the Termith on my account," said Marelle, "that will be the shroud for your soul, for all that your body might prosper."

"Not the Hainst or the Termith," replied Cete. "Some other clan. The Antach will tell me who his allies are, who I can serve safely and with honor. If I leave here, he will want me placed as well as possible—the Antach clan will need friends in the city clans. We won a great victory, but the enemies of the Antach will not give up their war."

Marelle took her hand from Cete's shoulder, and sat herself down in the chair opposite. "I don't know," she said. "If you will choose, I will go with your choice. Whichever you choose, it would be easier to be led than to decide. To be Marelle Antach, wife to the eighth in line to the Antach? But oh, for a doctor who could cut these clouds from before my eyes! To see your face, and the sun and the moon! If we have children, Cete, I want to see their faces!"

They were silent together for a long time.

Finally, Marelle spoke. "When I was a little girl," she said, "we lived in Coardur the City. In my fifth year, my mother died. Every day that year, I went to the church, wearing my mourning hood, and I prayed with all my heart for God to give her back to me. The priest there was of the Baern school. He saw me weeping, and my mourning hood, and after the services one day, he came over and asked me what I was praying for.

"I told him, and for a time he stayed beside me, on the narrow bench. 'I do not know if God will hear your prayer or not,' he said. 'For I do not know the mind of God. But let no one tell you that it is wrong for you to ask this thing of him, and let no one tell you that he will not hear your prayer. It is well that you ask these things of God, and it is well that he hears you asking. Never lose your faith that God can grant your prayers, no matter what the world tells you about what God can and cannot do.' It was a good thing that he said, but as with everyone, I have stopped asking God for the impossible. And now he sets before us two tables, with an impossible meal upon each, and we are asked to choose."

It was long after the time for dinner, and the fire below the chimney was nothing but embers; they gave enough light that Cete could see the white of the shroud, and the black of the mantle, but little more. "Two tables," said Marelle, "and two garments. Which would you wear?"

"The same as you, I think," said Cete. "I choose both the shroud and the mantle; I would stay in the Reach."

"Yes," said Marelle. "It would be safer to take the long road into the cities, to live in a house with servants, to advise and train and never again smell blood in the air, never slip on gore-slick grass. To pretend that it never happened, that we do not have that weight to bear. But while you are right that it is better to live than to die, it is better to live well than live poorly, and while we have them, our lives in the Reach will be better worth living."

Cete stood. He reached across to his wife, and pulled her to her feet. "Would the Lady Antach care to accompany Lord Cete Antach to the roof of their manor?"

She threw her arms around Cete. "We are fools, aren't we?"

"We are," said Cete. "And the clouds have not yet reached the horizon. When they come, we will regret this."

"For a time," said Marelle. "And then we shall either die or triumph."

"Or both," said Cete. "Both at once, or first one and then the other."

They went up to the roof together, and made love upon Marelle's embroidery, both the shroud and the mantle.

Acknowledgments

I'd like to thank Moshe Newman, Marissa Lingen, and Jo Walton for their advice and insight while this story was in its beginning stages.

Thanks also to Carl Engle-Laird, Irene Gallo, and the rest of the staff at Tor.com, without whose hard work and dedication you would not be reading this book.

About the Author

Alter S. Reiss is an archaeologist and writer who lives in Jerusalem with his wife, Naomi, and their son, Uriel. He likes good books, bad movies, and old-time radio shows.

TOR·COM

Science fiction. Fantasy.
The universe.
And related subjects.

*

More than just a publisher's website, Tor.com
is a venue for **original fiction, comics,** and
discussion of the entire field of SF and fantasy,
in all media and from all sources. Visit our site
today—and join the conversation yourself.

CPSIA information can be obtained at www.ICGtesting.com
Printed in the USA
LVOW06s1951240915

455596LV00003B/101/P